The Chronicles of Henson

Paul John Hausleben

Cover design and concept by Paul John Hausleben
All photographs by Paul John Hausleben
Scripture reference is from the King James Version, Holy Bible, public domain

Published by God Bless the Keg Publishing
Somewhere, U.S.A.

ISBN: 978-0-9986300-4-5

This is a work of fiction. Names, characters, businesses, places, events and incidents are either the product of the author's eccentric, strange and unusual imagination or used in a fictitious manner. Any resemblance to actual persons, living or dead or actual events is purely coincidental and it was not the intention of the author.

Dedication

To all the mysteries at Haunted Hall and to the cat, the dog, and the fire truck

The Chronicles of Henson

Paul John Hausleben

Contents

Acknowledgements

Thank you to my family and friends for the love and support during my endless writing adventures. Thank you to Mr. Mark Knopfler OBE for the amazing songs, "Tunnel of Love" and "Golden Heart," which on a late Saturday evening in October 2017, mixed with some mysterious liquid and provided me with layers of remarkable inspiration for writing the short story contained herein, "The Silver Locket." I would especially like to thank those readers who wrote to me and told me how much they enjoy the character of Paul John Henson. Thank you, and please know that without your notes and inspiration, this book would not exist.

"I will always be here. In the dark and in the light. The happy times and the sad times, the desperate times, always and forever, I am always here. God will not allow me to be anywhere else."

Paul John Hausleben

01 September 2108

Preface from the Author

Of my many characters, the character of Paul John Henson has been my most versatile character. Henson, in his various incarnations, details and participates in some of my most enjoyable times as a writer. It seems as if I can drop Henson into anything and the character thrives! Whether it is as a professional ice hockey player, or a Lutheran pastor or a Lutheran bishop, or just plain, old ordinary, Henson, the character is adaptable and consistent.

Time for honesty here.

At times, his creator and the author of these stories find Henson to be rather annoying! Other times, Henson grows on me and I feel a connection to Henson as he weaves his way through the many stories and adventures. Despite my best efforts to bury him, Henson resurrects repeatedly. I guess his fate and mine remain strangely intertwined. Often, I feel as if it is finally the proper time that Henson goes away forever, yet, readers always tell me how much they enjoy the character of Paul John Henson. I guess, in his own way, he is a rather cool guy.

A little touch of character analysis from the creator might be in order here.

Henson is severely flawed; despite his success and his superior intelligence, he is full of self-doubts. Henson is courageous and fearless and he truly fears nothing, anyone, or anything. He even stands up to God without an ounce of fear in his soul. Yet, despite the tremendous pain and suffering that occurs within his life, he remains faithful to the mission. The trouble always is that for Henson, he is never entirely sure what the mission is.

Henson is bold and to a certain extent, his reluctance to admit that he serves God in his profession makes him even more flawed. Yet, his heart is full of love, and his soul, full of emotions. No one loves harder and with more emotion than Henson does! My goal in writing this work was to depict Henson as human, as just a man, despite his profession. Often, we tend to put the clergy on a lofty pedestal and my desire was for Henson to display and admit his flaws, sins, and his humanism. After all, Henson loves to quote the Bible verse about how Jesus wept to show how Jesus was very much just a man. A human.

The emotions and his intelligence make him a great narrator and a keen observer to all the aspects of his life, his loved ones and the adventures. He is painfully honest and his details are accurate and concise and never embellished or subtracted from or altered. Henson records both the negative aspects of life and the positive aspects equally. As often as he accurately details whenever he receives praise, for example, when he receives comments to his handsome appearance, or his intelligence, he counters it with harsh criticism too. In fact, Henson might be his own harshest critic as he never denies, or sugarcoats, or misses a chance, to record the criticisms he receives, such as when his best friend, Mr. Harry M. Redmond Junior needles and labels Henson as an "Old Lady." Henson does not miss a trick and very much as Dr. Watson was to Sherlock Holmes, his keen observation skills and a penchant for observing and detailing everything, make Henson an interesting and fun character.

His effortless and intricately detailed narration of *The Adventures of Harry and Paul* is priceless. There, as the faithful and dedicated sidekick to the bombastic character of Harry M. Redmond Junior, his narration and their profound friendship made Henson the perfect spoon to the fork of Harry. You cannot help but to connect with Henson as he drags his heart and his faithfulness through, as he so often says, "The twists and turns of life."

While it is not a prerequisite to reading this book certain, aspects of the stories will flow better if the reader has read the novel, *Heaven's Gain*. After the novel, *Heaven's Gain*, I purposely left many holes in the story lines and various aspects of the character's adventures, and with this book; I decided to fill readers in on some of them.

Well, dear reader, here is where you find out some aspects of what was going on with Henson. That is the amazing aspect of the character of Paul John Henson in the fact that to readers, as well as to a certain extent, this author too, the character takes on an almost surreal presence. As if he is a real person.

Here in this collection, Henson is the star of the show and he details, to a great extent, what he calls his "Chronicles." For Henson, now, his writing becomes his last resort and greatest comfort as he works hard to release the "Ghosts" that he reports, continually haunt his life and his soul.

As always, consistent with either his narration, or his writings, the hidden message from Henson is that the root of life and all of religion is really all about love. Dear reader, love him or despise him, who can really argue with Henson on that one?

I hope that you enjoy reading this collection of stories as much as I have enjoyed writing them. Thank you for reading them.

Paul John Hausleben

01 September 2108

Prologue

It was summer vacation, and I was driving my mother and my sister crazy. It was only the week after the Fourth of July holiday and I think that Mum was ready to send me back to school already. First, it was sheets of paper, and then it was pencils, then two pieces of brown construction paper and finally, some tape and a stapler. Mum fetched all the supplies, and I went to work on the kitchen table. Assembling the brown construction paper for the front and rear cover of my "book" and then carefully slipping the sheets of paper inside of the covers and taping them and stapling them all together in a makeshift binding. For a seven-year-old kid, it was a reasonably solid effort.

Then, as Mum and Gramps shared tea and freshly baked scones at the table, and Mum ironed the old man's work shirts, prepared dinner, and folded laundry, I wrote and wrote inside of my "book."

Mum tried to sneak a peek of the "story" as did Gramps, but it was a secret.

"Not yet, Mum! Not yet, Gramps!" I howled in protest. "When it is done!"

When you are seven years old and a budding author on the cusp of greatness, you cannot give away any plot lines. When the story was complete, I searched and found my sister and convinced her to stop playing dress up with her dolls to draw the characters for my book.

"Ah, please, Dottie. You are older and you draw better than I do. I stink at drawing!"

My sister frowned and made me promise to play dress up later with her if she did it, and I fervently agreed to her terms.

My sister drew the illustrations under my careful watch and instructions.

"First a cat goes here, Dottie. Then his food dish here, and the sun and the clouds, and over here, please draw a doggie. Yup, right here. Then, on this page, draw a big car and a fire truck and then the cat on the back of the fire truck." Dottie sighed, but because she loved me, my dear sister drew onward, page after page.

"Right here goes a ghost."

"A ghost?" Dottie asked.

"Yup, a ghost. They are all around here. Can't you see them?"

"No. You are nuts, Paulie."

Dottie drew the ghost floating above the cat and the dog and the fire truck. Done! I grinned like a Halloween pumpkin. After fulfilling my dress-up obligation and even allowing Dottie to put a hat and lipstick on me, I joyfully ran and showed dear Mum my masterpiece.

"Oh my, I like the title, Paulie. The Mystery of Haunted Hall."

I nodded, smiled, and said, "By Paul John Henson. Dottie drew the pictures because I stink at drawing. I am a writer, not a drawer."

"An artist and an author, Paulie. The correct words are an artist and an author."

"Oh, okay, well, I wrote it, so I put my name on the front cover." I looked up and studied my mother's eyes for clues as to what she thought of my literary masterpiece.

"I see that . . . it is very . . . nice."

"Yup, wait until you read about the ghost."

"A ghost? Oh my, you do have quite the imagination, Paulie. Where do all of these stories come from all of the time?"

Mum then looked at me. She squinted her eyes and shook her head and asked me, "I am almost afraid to ask this, but why do you have lipstick on, Paulie?"

Therefore, the mission began.

I wrote, I wrote, and I never stopped.

And neither did the ghosts.

Letter One

Beloved Wife,

"I will lift up mine eyes . . . ah, well; you know the rest of the Psalm, dear Binky. Yet, right after you left us, the hills remained so barren.

No help was there.

I felt as if God not only voided our deal, but that I was a fool for following the plan to begin with.

Oh, my love, my beloved Binky, I was a mess! Mired in misery, anger, and hate, surrounded by those same bloody awful ghosts that have never left me alone, and spending my days drinking my soul into exile and my mind into oblivion. In my misery, I made many poor choices and did many things that I am not proud of now, or honestly, that I was not proud of even then. Then, with our children's help, with the intelligence, love, and guidance that they inherited from you, they awakened me from my foolishness and shook me from my anger, and despite my anger and reluctance, once more, I picked my sorry and worn-out ass off the charred remains of my soul, stuck my head out and followed the plan. As the situation evolved, I realized once again that God's plan for us might not, or in fact, ever, be what we want or desire, but to follow it faithfully, it takes immense courage and the understanding that the gift of God's Grace will only arrive, if you follow the plan faithfully. You would have thought that as a pastor, my own training would have kicked in and I would have been smart enough to follow what I preached for all of these years.

I think that Harry and your father were both correct when they said, "All those blows to my head from hockey pucks, scrambled my brains!"

Now, years after you became our loss and Heaven's gain, it is quite clear to me. I think that you needed to go before me into Heaven, to plow the road! Convince the saints, prophets, and wisdom of the Holy Spirit that despite my faults, I really did try!

Oh dear, Binky! How my pride overflows! Our children and grandchildren's lives are glorious, Rose misses Harry as I miss you, and collectively we miss you both. Yet, there is also an understanding in Rose's heart. Together, Rose and I, with our combined love for God and each other, we join forces to carry out the plan. In honor and in the glory of not only our beloved spouses and friends, but in honor of the Grace bestowed on us.

There is little doubt, at least to me there is—that there is so much more for me to do here before I join you. I feel it every day. I write as if I am a madman. Often, the words cannot leave my mind quickly enough. It is the same as when the flow overcame me in hockey, and there was no way a puck could slip by me into the goal.

As Harry and you would say so often, "Not a marble can roll by you, number twenty-seven. Not a marble." Well, my beloved Binky, it works in my compositions too.

Please look around at the glorious office where I sit and write. Our beloved daughter, Heather Sarah, set this all up for me, for us. Heather Sarah knows me all too well, and she even had a wet-bar installed for me. It is within crawling distance of my desk for those long writing marathons that mix with a few glasses of a fine Scotch to create glorious, but painful writing adventures. You know better than anyone does that where I write is of such importance to me. This glorious office is such a far cry from the little desk that we had in the corner of our first house there in Great Falls. Yet, the little desk remains carefully preserved in the corner of this office. I keep some of my original sermons in a folder upon the desktop. A reminder of the fact that where we begin is often not far from where we end. Where we rest our heart and our love is to where we will always return.

For some strange reason, the writing gives me solace. Not only in the writing of my books, and the detailing of the endless adventures of Harry and Paul and all the rest of us, or in some religious writings, but in writing these letters to you. Letters that I know you read because I feel you watching over my shoulder right now as I compose them. It seems foolish, or at least on the surface it does. Foolish to compose letters to you, my wife, a wife who now is a Lutheran saint in Heaven, but I have never been conventional.

No sense in changing now!

It is a cleansing exercise for both my mind and my soul and the words have to come out as I carry on with whatever the work is that God, Rose, our children, and our loved ones here on Earth assign to me.

In many ways, it has become my purpose, my mission, to detail what I now call, "The Chronicles of Henson." Some are emotional, some are silly, some as you know, are quite unbelievable, but true! As of late, I write differently. Differently, since you left us and since I have now completed writing and detailing many, if not most of, the adventures of Harry and Paul and of our lives together. I write of my adventures while performing my pastoral duties and I write of the many people, situations, and emotions that I encountered.

I write within a magnificent outpouring of my soul, the words manifested within my own memories and emotions, inspired by the haunting of so many of these ghosts that surround me. The ghosts refuse to allow me to ignore them. They float everywhere that I look and it is much the same as it was when I was a little boy and wrote that first book on my summer vacation from school. The ghosts sit right next to me until I release them to haunt the pages of these many books. In retrospect, I am glad to provide a release for them and for me too.

In the end, I write for you, for our love, and mainly, to feel you next to me.

Now and forever.

Love always,

#27

The Hallway

Mr. Walter Kenny was a long-time parishioner of Reunion Lutheran Church. I must say, I very much enjoyed his company. He was an engaging man, with clear blue eyes, a thick tuft of snow-white hair, a quick smile and he found it very easy to laugh and share his quick wit. Perhaps Walter's feelings reciprocated toward me, or he was a grand actor in that he seemed to enjoy my company too, because we shared many interesting discussions over the years that I served as the Senior Pastor of Reunion Lutheran Church.

On the other hand, perhaps, he simply humored me that he enjoyed my company.

Perhaps.

I did choose to call him my friend, as well as a parishioner. I think in my heart that he felt the same feelings toward me.

Walter was in many of my Bible study classes and he dutifully served on many committees in various functions for the church. We would often speak of sports. Walter, as my own father was, remained a dedicated baseball fan and he too, as did my old man, lived, breathed and loved the New York Bugs. Walter enjoyed hearing of my tales of playing professional hockey, and while he knew little of the intricacies of the sport, it seemed as if the stories of my years of battles on the ice sparked his competitive juices for sport. Sometimes, he invited me to speak and chat with his pals at the local Veteran's Club and I would sit, listen, and share a few beers with his pals, and with Walter, as they told me many amazing tales of their experiences in the military. Much more so than most parishioners of Reunion Lutheran Church, I knew most of his life story. As I grew older, it became a practice of mine to take careful notes during these special times, not only to get to know the person or persons involved but also to use the stories and experiences in some of my potential writings later on down the road. The pastor in me told me to share in the lives of the flock, and the writer in me, told me to be very cognizant of the experiences of everyone and not allow the stories of their lives to escape my mind, my pen, or my heart.

While I drove the distance to visit Mr. Kenny in the Lutheran nursing home that was now his residence, I ran the story of his life through my mind. Seldom, if ever, did I take written notes; instead, God granted me an amazing gift to retain all the information within my mind. Ironically, the exact gift which had escaped Walter Kenny, was now my strong point.

Now, let me pay attention to the roadways, but run the notes in my mind.

Will the memories be verbatim? No, I do not think that my mind can flip those newsreels, but I needed to recall as much of his life as I could manage to conjure up.

Here we go now and if I recall it all correctly, we were sharing a beer or two while sitting at an old oak bar in the basement of the Veteran's Hall.

Walter served his country gallantly in World War Two. He served seven years in the United States Navy, assigned during his entire enlistment to the Silent Service in the era of diesel submarines and mayhem.

No doubt, that, through and through, from his pea coat to his pancake hat, to his polished, black, low-quarters, that he was a submariner. During his years of service, Walter achieved the rank of a Petty Officer, First Class, with a rate of a torpedo man on a Tang Class submarine, which engaged in many rounds of combat with the Japanese in the Pacific Theatre of the war.

Walter always emphasized that it was an old diesel boat and not one of those, "Fancy-ass nuke jobs."

His service was anything but a walk in the park, seeing the world gloriously while gleefully sailing the high seas while traveling port-to-port!

Hell no!

Walter saw more than his share of hellfire and horror, and he shared tales of horror with me and with his many friends. Walter's boat was depth-charged, attacked from virtually every known weapon, device, craft, and airplane contained within the Japanese arsenal; they endured harrowing escapes and a near-miss survival from a kamikaze attack and narrowly escaped aircraft gunfire that strafed the deck of their boat when they surfaced one day for some glorious fresh air. No, Walter had seen the horrors of war and tasted all too closely the taste of gunpowder rimmed with the prospect of death. He had held fellow sailors in his arms while they died from their wounds, and he cried at the loss of his comrades. The horrors of war never left his mind, and I doubted that they ever would do so. What a man can do to a fellow man is often inconceivable.

"You are a city kid too, Pastor Paul, so you can relate. Can you, or could you, ever imagine, I mean, for a young man from the tumultuous streets of Newark, New Jersey the horror of squishing to death within a can, made of steel, while sinking to the bottom of the ocean?"

In an answer to his profound question, I shook my head, to indicate that, no, that would be something that I could never imagine being my end fate. The city streets of my youth, and beyond, held little visions of submarines for any of us.

Death by gunshot was entirely more realistic.

I shared in the fact that this method of dying was not Walter's picture-perfect idea of how he should meet his final demise. What Walter saw, what his experiences consisted of and what he managed to endure, were, in my opinion, experiences that no one could categorize, identify, or even quantify in any manner. Unless you were there, it was impossible to understand. Now, years later, long after the experiences, honestly, after the knee-knocking fear, long after the remnants of the adrenalin expired, and when the mission long since ended, Walter Kenny was still proud and honorable of the mission.

He was a proud United States Navy veteran.

In his opinion, he told me many times that Walter Kenny was simply a survivor.

I had little doubt that Walter was an honorable man and a man proud of his service, but even prouder of the collective commitment that his fellow submariners and boat-mates contributed to preserve freedom. Freedom, for not only his country but also, in his judgment and within his perception, for the entire world. If Walter missed anything within his life, he missed the faces, the smiles, and the voices of the men that he served with in the Silent Service. The bravest of the brave. Men who stared down the potential of death every day, men of audacity and men of honor.

They made up his soul.

They made up his heart.

Walter never left the Silent Service; he simply did not physically report to a boat for duty any longer.

As far as serving, Walter still served and, in his heart, he always would serve. He told me glorious thoughts of how remarkable it was to smell the sea air when the boat finally surfaced. To feel the warmth of the sun on your face, when you had not seen it in what seemed as if it was forever, and at some point, you wondered if you would ever see it again. Standing at attention in dress whites, while on deck as they cruised victoriously into port, all of these memories forever embedded in his mind. Walter often told me of his pride, and the picture of Walter and his comrades standing on the deck of their boat, while sailing into port, painted vivid strokes of glory within my own mind. It was a glorious memory of which Walter proudly shared with me and I am very grateful to Walter for having done so.

After the war, Walter returned to his home city, married his high school sweetheart, and he found work in a shipping corporation. Walter's leadership skills and knowledge of the world, combined with his superior organizational skills, landed Walter in the traffic and distribution department on the warehouse side of the corporation. Walter enjoyed the work, and the corporation treated their employees rather well. The old submariner remained as dedicated to his civilian job as he had to his country during his military days, and Walter rose quickly through the ranks. Before too many years, Walter Kenny received a promotion to Director of Traffic and Distribution, he was in charge of the management of the entire warehouse operation, trafficking paperwork, shipping manifests, and soon, the entire shipping operation of the corporation fell under Walter's guidance. He excelled at his job; Walter earned respect and remained upbeat and positive during even the most stressful of times.

"I credit the United States Navy, Pastor Paul, for keeping me calm under fire. After all, a lost shipment of products is nothing like having depth charges landing on your head."

I could understand his point.

Despite the horrors of war that he faced, Walter remained jolly, a man with a grand sense of humor and a man who knew very well how it is so easy to take our lives for granted and then watch as it all disappears in a flash. Before too long, Walter sat in a corner office and directed his operations. There he stayed until he retired after over forty years of service with the company. He told me how on the walls of his office were many pictures of his boat, his fellow sailors, and of his wife. A wife who tragically passed away from cancer after they had only been married for ten years or thereabouts. Just about the time that Walter received his promotion and about the time that he felt that he could afford to buy a fancy house and give his glorious wife all the finer things that he felt his wife deserved, she was gone. I never had the pleasure to meet her, but after all the discussions and love shared between us; I think that I knew her quite well.

"She was the love of my life, Pastor Paul, spectacularly gorgeous. We never had time to start a family, and now, I have no one left on this side of Heaven. We are both men, and you are my pastor, so I can speak openly . . . she had a body like a goddess and when we made love, my world turned inside and out too. I can never remarry. I am a one-woman-man. Forever. I still weep for her at least once a week. I guess that I always will weep for her love. My wife had a voice soft as silk, a heart full of love and compassion, and the world is such a better place because of my wife. I honestly believe that to be true."

While turning off the highway and gliding on the off-ramp for the exit that I needed to take, I smiled once again at the memory of recalling how I glowed at his immense love and his honest statement, which proudly broadcasted the depth of his love for his wife. When the stop light at the end of the ramp turned red, and I pulled my ancient jeep to a gentle stop, I recalled the next question that Walter asked of me. In my mind, it sparked so many more memories in my heart, kind of as if it was the epitome of my adventures. Walter asked the question, which began what I now call, "The Chronicles of Henson." The same question that actually began my long journey in this life to fulfill what God's plan for me actually was. It was not hockey, no, despite my inner desires and the longing in my heart to capture what the sport gave to me and taught me. No, professional hockey was not my ultimate path. The sport was exactly as many people foretold it to me, many, many times, "Just a vehicle to ride in for some time." No, instead, it was the same question that I asked to the Redmond's family Catholic priest and my good friend, Father Mark O'Brien, when my best friend, Harry M. Redmond Junior's beloved and loved wife, Sky Blu, passed away. The question, which changed my life and my destiny.

"Why?" Walter asked me, after a long sip of the brew and with a lick of tears in the corners of his eyes. "I have to think that I have faith, praise the Lord and all the Major Prophets too. Kinda been a decent man, made some stupid-ass, bone head moves here and there, some stuff that I am not too proud of, like, shacking up with a weird woman and having wild sex on her kitchen floor when I was in port one day, comes to my mind, but still, all in all, I am not a bad man. I love God, ask for forgiveness, and acknowledge my bone-headedness. Is that a word?"

I smiled at his wit, but shrugged my shoulders at the question.

Walter continued, "I read my Bible, love Reunion Lutheran Church and respect your guidance, and I thank God every day for what I have and all that I am. Still, I have to ask. Why? Why did God take my beloved wife so early?"

THE QUESTION.

Now, I could have answered The Question, in many ways, perhaps, borrowing upon Father Mark's glorious words to me of so long ago, but instead, I used Walter Kenny's own words and added Father Mark's poignancy to them.

With a gentle glint of a smile, and with words from deep within and amongst the Chronicles of Henson, Pastor Paul answered, The Question, "Because you weep for her love.

Because your wife had a voice soft as silk, a heart full of love, compassion, and most of all, because Heaven is such a better place because of your wife. I honestly believe that to be true. Love is God's greatest gift to us."

Walter Kenny wiped the tears away, mumbled a thank you and then asked me, "For a pastor with long hair and a beard who looks like some weird hippie, you are always right on target. So, how 'bout another beer, Pastor Paul?"

The driveway leading to the Lutheran nursing home was a long one. Once parked, it was a short walk to the lobby.

"I have signed the logbook. I will visit Mr. Kenny, but first, I am going to slip into the chapel for a quick prayer."

An attractive young woman working the front desk of the Lutheran nursing home looked up from her paperwork, flipped her hair to smooth her curls out a bit, smiled and answered, "Okay, Pastor Paul. You know the way. Right?"

"I do."

"And you know that Mr. Kenny is now in the memory-care wing. Right? Do you have your identification card and pass card?"

I smiled, pointed to the card dangling around my neck on a lanyard that was too long and waved, while answering, "I do and I do. Thank you."

I caught her first glance at the card and then to my face. A coy smile appeared on her face.

Oh, oh!

"And do you know my home address and have my cell phone number?"

I stopped short for a brief second or two, until I realized that her words along with the coy smile meant that she was flirting with me, or teasing me, or a combination thereof.

"Sorry, I cannot help it. Seriously, anything for you, Pastor Paul. I still cannot believe that with all that hair and good looks, you are a Lutheran minister or, in fact, a bishop. How I wish that you would take my phone number."

Technically, the young woman was correct. I now served as the Bishop for the Northeast District of the synod. I had been coming here for a few years now since Walter moved in, first, in the nursing assistance section and now that his disease progressed, in the memory care section. This young woman, as well as many others, knew not to call me, "Bishop Henson."

Too stuffy. Pastor Paul worked for all of these years, no reason to change my title now.

While I paused in my steps, I ran the various options for an appropriate response through my mind and after an inventory of them; I decided that a smile and no verbal response would be the best response of all. The young woman seemed harmless enough, even if she was not entirely appropriate for her somewhat suggestive behavior toward a clergyman, but nonetheless, harmless.

Henson might be many things, but I am not a prude.

At the end of the last pew in the row of pews, I set aside my carrying case with the items that I brought with me for Mr. Kenny. The chapel was empty, just the Chancel Lamp fueled by oil with a flame that flickered at me, while hanging above and to the rear of the pulpit, just beyond the altar rail. I did not bother turning on any lights. The sunlight through the stained-glass windows worked well enough; besides, I always thought that praying works better in the dark. That might be my imagination, but I have stuck with the theory for all of these years and, while obscure, I remained entitled to my own unsubstantiated opinion. With a slow and painful kneel, a crack in my knees and a twitch in my lower back, I not so gracefully descended to the kneeling bench below the altar rail. Those hockey injuries were now all catching up to me in droves.

"Lord, guide me in my words, in my actions and in my work for the Kingdom of Heaven. I ask you for forgiveness of my many transgressions and for your assistance in the shepherding of Mr. Walter Kenny and any other person who might require my meager attempts at comfort in their times of need. In Jesus' name, we pray. Amen."

The ascension from the bench was not too graceful either. While holding my lower back, which suddenly became very tight and painful with a lower back spasm, I performed a quick bow at the cross, mounted behind the front altar, I made the sign of the cross, and Pastor Paul John Henson was on his way. In my haste to see Mr. Kenny, I almost forgot my case. Honestly, I often wonder these days if I might be in the early stages of forgetfulness as a prelude to what now ails Mr. Kenny and so many others living within this home. Yet, upon close self-examination, I knew in my heart that it was not a disease that afflicted me, nor was it a prelude to one and I had to agree with my friends and my faithful assistant, Ms. Martha Wiggins that this was simply a result of overwork and some exhaustion due to my chronic insomnia. It was not that I did not sleep; it was that I slept in short, broken patterns. My mind never stopped. Either my mind searched for words and stories to write, or the ghosts of my past and some present haunted my thoughts. In an effort to avoid the flirtatious young woman on duty in the lobby, and in an effort to convince my hockey-worn body that those creaks and cracks of the joints were due to inactivity, I slipped into the staircase opposite the Chapel. In order to reach the elevators, I had to walk past her and no doubt; she was listening for my footsteps and the climb will do me good. Loosen me up.

While I climbed, I thought of my mission here.

Around six or so years earlier, when Mr. Walter Kenny first received the diagnosis of dementia and then the doctor pronounced his affliction to be a full-blown Alzheimer's disease, Mr. Kenny moved quickly to put things in order. Since he had no living relatives, he hired an attorney for his estate planning and then asked me to be involved, not only as the Executor of his will, but as his friend and his guardian, too. Walter had worked long and very hard and he lived frugally and he saved wisely. He had an extensive estate, both in real estate, money, and investments, and in anticipation of his final fate; he made sure that he gifted to Reunion Lutheran Church a great deal of his estate. The lawyer advised Mr. Kenny of how the process would eventually work and as his condition deteriorated and a nursing home became his permanent and final residence, the estate planning paid off handsomely. Reunion Lutheran Church benefitted from Mr. Kenny's generosity and his wise planning, paid for his long-term care too.

"Unless, on purpose, I guess we can never pick the method of our own demise, but this wretched disease, gives me the worst of thoughts, Pastor Paul," Walter rather tragically told me one day shortly after his diagnosis. "To think that it will steal my thoughts and my memory is a little difficult to grasp. I hope that it never steals the memories of my wife and all that we shared, my Navy experiences and the faces and voices of my fellow sailors. Most of all, I hope that it never steals all of my dreams. It can take some of them, but please, I ask that it leaves me just a few to recall. Like riding off into the last sunset while on the deck of my final submarine cruise. You know, while dressed in my finest dress whites, the smell of the sea in the air, a little salt spray and a whiff of diesel fuel in my nose. My wife, Maggie, will be waiting for me when we make port. I will give her the biggest kiss that I ever gave to her. You see, Pastor Paul, even at my age, I hold on to my dreams. I think it is important to do so. When it becomes terrible and I just sit and stare at the shadows on the wall of my room, promise me you will come by and try to give me my dreams and memories back to me. Will you please do that for me, Pastor Paul?"

I extended my hand and warmly grasped his hand and shook it hard. "I will, of course, I promise. You can count on me."

"I know that I can. You are an exceptional man, Pastor Paul. Not only a man of God, and our pastor, but also you are a remarkable friend. I wish that I had known you for all of my life. Perhaps, I have, and we just do not realize it. Honestly, it feels as if that is the case. Maybe we have known each other for even longer. Right?"

As I did with the lobby gal, I recalled how I had run the various options for an appropriate response through my mind and after an inventory of them; I decided that a smile and no verbal response would be the best response of all.

With just a bit of huff 'n' puff, I arrived on the floor where the Memory Care Wing of the home was located and peered through the viewing windows of the door. A long hallway loomed in front of me.

A very long, somewhat sad, hallway.

Rooms dotted the hallway, some doors open, some doors closed, but the rooms lined the hallway as if they were silent enclaves of bliss for the patients to retreat to for peace.

Safe ports within a violent storm.

A few of the less ambulatory patients sat in wheelchairs and they silently slumped over their bodies and drooled on their shirts, blouses, and dresses, or gently used their feet as paddles to propel their way around and up and down the hallway. Before entering the hallway, I checked for the proximity of the patients to the door because the wheelchairs had alarms on the chairs to warn the caretakers and nurses as to a potential escape by one of the patients. If the chair ventured close to the door, the alarm sounded. The door area of the hallway was clear and with a swipe of my pass card on the reader, the door happily beeped and slowly opened. The opening of the doors caused a happy response to the patients in the hallway.

A visitor is often an exciting event!

Such a simple thing, such as a door opening, a person

entering and walking down the hallway, which is an event that we all have experienced countless times throughout our lives, now becomes an exciting event. Sad, but amazing, all in one rather stunning, lump dose of reality.

I walked the hallway quickly. A few patients pretended that they knew me and I stopped by each one, and smiled at them, and asked them how they felt. I picked up a stuffed doggie from the floor that one elderly woman always clutched, and I placed it back into her gnarled hands.

She gloriously accepted it and mumbled to me, "I lost Joey when we went for a walk. I am so happy that he came home! Did he bark at the back door to be let in the kitchen?"

"He did," I said, while I set my case down on the floor, brushed my long hair back over my shoulders and knelt down next to her wheelchair. I watched her gray eyes study my face, and then they traveled to the wooden cross around my neck. She reached out and carefully touched and felt the white pastor's collar around my neck. For a long time, I felt her running the material through her fingers, while I studied the lines of her face and the emptiness of her eyes for clues as to what faint memory that the collar could have invoked for this gentle soul.

There was none.

Finally, she let go and smiled at me. I smiled at her too, blessed her and made the sign of the cross on her forehead, and stood up while she waved and gently paddled her feet in an effort to turn her wheelchair up the hallway. Her efforts were futile; she had little in the way of strength left, so I gave her a gentle push in order to help her on her way.

"I have to take Joey to the park. Is the park this way?"

I pointed and told her with some element of assurance in my voice, "It is. That way."

Off the two of them journeyed down the hallway.

To the park.

After picking my case back up, I walked slowly down the hallway, studying the patients along the way; I smiled at those who were somewhat conscious and stopped to pray and convey a general blessing to those asleep or unconscious of their surroundings.

Even though I had traveled down this hallway many times during my tenure in service as pastor of Reunion Lutheran Church, and now as the bishop, for some reason, I never noticed the hallway, as I did today, at least, not with this type of perception. I had to think to myself, what a collection of sad and lost souls massed here in this hallway. For some reason, today, it was more humbling than it was heart wrenching. To think of what these people all did during their lives, the careers they had, the families they raised, the people they loved, the experiences they all had, now, to end up in this hallway, mindlessly counting and passing time, chasing shadows on the floors and on the walls, remained beyond the comprehension and control of my thoughts.

While walking, I prayed.

One poor chap, whom I had not ever seen in the hallway before today, sat prone in a long, special wheelchair of some sort—it was almost as if it was a bed with wheels, bent at a certain angle, and the patient dropped inside as if he was a cork in a bottleneck. He sat along the edge of the hallway, not moving much. His back seemed as if it would not allow his body to fold and sit and he said not a single word, but instead, he studied me with his eyes. I walked over to him and he slowly reached out his hand, which I took and gently grasped it. His body odor was immense, the poor chap smelled terrible, as if he was soaked full of gallons of urine, and his breath smelt as if it was a combination of wet socks mixed with a wet dog's fur.

I did not mind, and I asked, "How are you today? I am Pastor Paul John Henson. Can you tell me your name?"

He simply shook my hand, stared at my face, and said

not a word.

I looked up and saw a familiar face. I spotted Sharon, the home's most reliable (in my opinion) and dedicated caretaker. Sharon was a nurse's aide, and she conveniently was walking down the hallway in my direction. I waved her over.

She smiled at me and made her way over while saying, "Hi. What can I do for you today, Pastor Paul?"

"Hello, thank you. This poor chap needs mountains of attention. Seems as if he is having an extra difficult time today."

She studied the man and her nose told her the balance of the story.

"Oh yes, I see and smell it, too. Thank you. Sorry, but it has been an extra difficult day today. Many troubles with the gang, but now, things have settled down and they are mostly all relaxed and in the hallway. I need to check the phases of the moon because everyone was so disturbed earlier today."

"I see. No apology is necessary. I cannot even imagine how you do all that you do. Do you need any assistance? I can take him to his room and bathe him if you need me to do so. I can help if you are shorthanded today."

They were always shorthanded and while the home did the best they could, staffing was always a challenge here.

Low pay, hard work, long hours . . . it had to be more than just a job, it needed to be a mission.

I knew the feeling.

"Oh no, thank you, Pastor Paul. I know that you would help. Margie told me what you did last week for her. I am fine. We actually have extra hands today. I have Bruce covered."

"Okay. Bruce. That is his name, eh? Thank you, Sharon." I turned my gaze and words to Bruce's direction, "Bruce, my friend, listen, please. Sharon is going to take care of you. Clean you up a bit. That will feel good. Right?"

Bruce did not even react to my words. I wondered if somewhere deep in his haze if he was painfully aware of his own smell and condition. By the grip he had on my hand, I had to think that he was aware of it. On the other hand, perhaps, it was my imagination that he was. His mind seemed empty, but I think Bruce's soul remained locked within him. Regardless, Bruce still held my hand, so I gently pried my hand loose from his as Sharon worked the wheel locks loose on his chair and moved him down the hallway.

While wheeling Bruce away, Sharon told me, "Walter has been a hot and wild mess today. He is still in his bed, Pastor Paul. We were praying for your early arrival. We know you always visit on Thursday afternoon, so we did not call you. I hope you can calm him down a bit. As of the last few days, he stays in bed and we cannot place him in the hallway. I am afraid it is becoming sadder with each passing day."

I nodded, but stood there in the hallway with my case in my hand, waiting for a bit more to go on in order for me to help Walter. Sensing my searching, Sharon spoke while moving farther down the hallway, in the direction of what I presumed to be Bruce's room. I thought how it must be the last room left, since she was rapidly running out of the hallway.

That seemed so profound because this hallway of lost souls seemed endless.

"He has been calling out endlessly to get rid of Hoppleburger, because he is terrible. I have no idea who Hoppleburger is, or was, but I hope you can rid Walter of him."

At the mention of the name "Hoppleburger," I could not help but to laugh aloud. For me, the memories that the name invoked caused not only laughter but also just a hint or two of sadness. I recalled my old man ranting endlessly as to how his baseball nemesis, the shortstop for his beloved New York Bugs, Billy "The Banjo" Hoppleburger, was a hopeless and hapless, "Bum!"

Sharon smiled, but since she did not understand, she asked, "Ah, okay, Pastor Paul? Forgive me, but what the hell is a Hoppleburger? Do you know of him, or it, or whatever?"

"Yes, I know him and of him, yes, Hoppleburger, was an old-time baseball player. A shortstop for the New York Bugs and in my own father's opinion and apparently, in Walter's opinion too, he was a bum."

Sharon laughed, stopped wheeling Bruce and carefully maneuvered his special chair into the doorway of his room, while replying, "I see. I think. Weird, how that memory came up today. Good luck with that, Pastor Paul. Good luck."

"Thanks. You too."

I walked up the hallway to Walter's room.

Room number 415.

I stopped and looked at the glass display case mounted on the wall right outside Walter's room. Each room had a case. The case faced the hallway and the purpose of each display case was to contain a biography about each patient and mementos of their lives. Some cases up and down the hallway had many items in them. Loving preservation of a person's life. Photographs, favorite sports teams, pictures of their homes, their families, their pets, parts and pieces of their lives.

Can you imagine?

It all came down to this with a person's entire life contained within a glass display case in the hallway.

Some rooms had nothing, or next to nothing, within their display case. Simply, the person's name and in some cases, their occupation and where they lived. Walter's case had a biography that I had typed up, and some United States Navy memorabilia, a collection of his military medals, some of his ribbons, and a picture of Walter and his gorgeous wife, Maggie. For an added touch, as well as some more insight into Walter's interests and life, I also added some New York Bug's memorabilia. No doubt that Hoppleburger would harbor deep and profound disappointment, if I did not add that touch to the case.

Today, my mission was that I intended to keep my promise to Walter. I remained surprised by Sharon's testimony that he was verbal today. As of late, the progress of the disease reached a peak where it stole most of his words. Walter seldom spoke and rarely recognized me anymore.

If ever.

In speaking with the hospice nurses and the doctor assigned to Mr. Walter Kenny, they all reported that his condition was rapidly declining. They added that in their opinion, from here on in, it was going to be a fast and brutal slide downhill.

Walking into Walter's room, I found him upright in his bed, propped up by some pillows behind his back. The television was on and yakking away. The television was only noise and flickering objects. Walter did not watch it or follow it. The nurses and caretakers used it as background noises to sooth his mind.

Walter was staring at all the shadows on the wall of his room.

It was all that he had left to do.

Yes, indeed, it was time to keep my promise to him.

"Hi, Walter. How are you today? What is this all about with this Hoppleburger stuff?"

Walter opened his eyes, and he searched the room to find me. His vision was failing now, too. He found me, slowly extended his hand out, and I set my case down and took his hand. The old sailor looked as if he wanted to answer me, but the words would not arrive.

"Do you know who I am?"

To my surprise, he nodded his head and softly

whispered, "Yes. You are Short-leg, Sandy Howell. Did you get rid of that horrible Hoppleburger? The banjo made two more errors in the game today. He cost us a win."

For a brief instant, I almost went along with Walter's thoughts and decided that I would pretend to be the old, long-time manager of the New York Bugs, "Short-leg," Sandy Howell. However, that would not be fair, instead - I told the truth. "No, I am not, Short-leg, Sandy Howell. I am Pastor Paul, but yes, Hoppleburger will not be playing for the Bugs team any longer."

Considering the fact that Hoppleburger retired about forty-five years ago, I felt better about not fudging the truth to Walter. He no longer expressed emotion, but I had to think that if he could smile, he would have. But his eyes lit up with my words and he nodded his head just a little. It seemed as if he was very quiet and calm now. I imagined that all of his yelling earlier in the day must have used up his words and energy.

I pulled up a chair next to his bed and one-by-one, I reached into the case that I brought and did my best to keep my promise to Walter of what was now, quite a few years ago. First, I pulled out and showed Walter a New York Bugs baseball cap. He stared at it, but he did not react. Then, I showed him pictures of Reunion Lutheran Church, a few pictures of him dressed in his Navy uniform, a picture of Maggie, a few words and explanations about his wife, and some talk about his place of employment. I even had found in his collection, when we cleaned out his home along with Lutheran Social Services, the program from his retirement party, along with a special plaque the company gave to Walter to honor his service.

No reaction.

None, what so ever.

I was not keeping my promise to invoke a memory for him when the battle was almost over and lost.

Under my breath, as I placed my hand around the last

object in my case, I said a prayer, for the Lord to help me, for the Lord to intervene and for one last memory, somehow to return.

I pulled out his dress white sailor's cap and gently took Walter's hand and placed the cap in his hand. His eyes studied it for a very long time. His fingers played with and ran over the anchor and naval insignia mounted on the front of the cap.

As Walter carefully studied the cap, I gently spoke to the old sailor with a variation of his own words. "Walter, this afternoon, you are riding off into a sunset while on the deck of your submarine. It is the end of a long cruise. You are dressed in your finest dress whites, the smell of the sea is in the air, a little salt spray and a whiff of diesel fuel is in your nose. Best of all, your wife, Maggie, is waiting for you when you make port. She will be thrilled to see you and I promise that you will give her the biggest kiss that you ever gave to her. You see, Walter, with the Lord's help and guidance, you will forever hold on to your dreams. I think it is important to do so."

Walter listened to my words; I knew in my heart that he did so. When I finished, he still held the cap tightly in his hands. He moved his head slowly and handed the cap back to me. I swear that there were tears in his eyes.

The Lord answered my prayer.

A low and weak voice, but audible.

"Maggie is gorgeous, Pastor Paul. You are a good friend to me. We have been friends forever. Maybe longer. Thank you."

I smiled, stood up, and placed the cap on his head. I hugged him warmly and whispered, "Yes, she is, Walter, and the best part, is that she waits for you. Honest, she does, because the world is a better place because of the life of Mr. Walter Kenny. And you, Walter, are my good friend too. Thank you for you."

Mission accomplished, and a promise kept.

Three weeks or so later, Mr. Walter Kenny's tour ended, and he sailed into his final port. Walter's dream of joining his beloved wife finally came to be a wonderful reality.

I held his hand as he died.

It was my honor to do so.

I noticed that the calendar on the wall in Walter's room was displaying the month of April.

It was May.

A few days after the funeral, I once again walked, The Hallway. This time, I stopped at each of the display cases and made a note of them all.

Each one in, The Hallway.

I did not miss any of them. Even the ones that had no items on display, but only had small biographies. I stopped and carefully and respectfully read each one. While walking The Hallway and studying the display cases, I tried hard to be polite to the patients in The Hallway. I did not want to ignore them, but today I wanted to honor them.

'Bruce Thomas Watson. Bruce is a retired civil engineer. Bruce is from North Arlington, New Jersey and he worked for over forty years as an engineer. Bruce built bridges.'

I moved on to the next one.

'Irene Margaret Van Dyke. Irene lived her entire life in East Paterson, New Jersey and taught third and fourth grade in the East Paterson Public Schools for forty-five years.'

I thought about the dedication, the lives that Irene touched, and the mountains of knowledge she conveyed to children and to the world. Slowly, I moved on to the next one.

'Millie Dawson. A retired nurse and dog lover. Her husband, Alexander, was a Lutheran pastor. Pastor Dawson died in 1982. They lived in Jersey City, New Jersey and they were married for sixty-two years.'

I thought how sixty-two years of marriage represents to

me an almost unimaginable love. To have known and to have loved one person for that long only glorifies God in the highest.

Love is God's greatest gift to us.

I stared at the picture of a beautiful young woman, dressed in a nurse's uniform, standing arm-in-arm with a pastor dressed in his black suit and white pastor's collar. The pastor was tall, proud, and very handsome. The handsome couple had a small dog at their feet.

Suddenly, my spine shivered, and I made the connection. I recalled the manner in which she fingered and studied my pastor's collar and how she held Joey, the stuffed dog. The memory caused Heaven to settle within my small part of Earth.

I moved on to the next one.

I had to make a solemn vow that I would not miss even one. Each one was as poignant as the previous one was.

The Hallway seemed endless, yet now The Hallway did not seem as if it was filled with lost souls. On the contrary, it seemed as if it overflowed with life, love, and golden memories.

Memories surpassed only by dreams.

Endless dreams in the endless hallway.

"Sharon, can I please have the key to the display case for Walter's room? I need to clean it out and pack away his belongings. I am sure that Room 412 will have a new resident in a few days."

Sharon nodded and looked at me with sad eyes as she reached into a drawer at the front desk.

"Of course, here is the key, Pastor Paul. There is some talk of a person moving into 412. I am sure in a few days it will have a new resident. They always arrive. Some are even sadder than the previous one."

Her eyes studied me as she added, "I guess that you must miss, Walter." After speaking, Sharon paused, and her eyes looked down and then returned to study my own eyes.

"Stupid thought, I am so sorry. I know that you do and I do, too. Do you realize that you visited him every Thursday for as long as I can recall? You truly are a man of God, and you were such a good friend to Walter. It was more than your duty as his pastor and as the bishop of this district. Yes, no doubt that it was so much more than just duty or a job to you. It was heartfelt and inspirational to all of us. Walter was more than just a parishioner to you and the church. Walter was your friend. We all could tell."

I took the key and nodded.

For the first time since Mr. Walter Kenny passed away, I felt a rim of tears lining my eyes and I had no shame in displaying the tears to Sharon. Years ago, life hardened me to the point where I could not cry, mourn, or lament.

Now, it seems as if that is all that I do.

She spotted my emotions overcoming me and the very kind woman came out from behind the desk and warmly hugged me.

"I am so sorry, Pastor Paul. I am so very sorry for your loss."

"He did so much in his life and it is all so amazing," I spoke and then paused to wipe the tears from my eyes.

The tears quickly returned.

"If I recall correctly, your own father died of Alzheimer's disease. I am so sorry."

"He did. It is devastating. It tears away pieces of your very soul. My father had a brilliant mind that shone as if it was a beacon. The disease captured his mind inside a shroud of mind-numbing fog. My father could take an automobile engine apart blindfolded. Tools in his hands were similar to the brush strokes of a great painter working in oils. A display of skill, awe and beauty. In the end . . . he could not use a key to unlock a door."

I looked away and down The Hallway and my eyes studied the collection of souls trapped inside the same shells of misery. My eyes went to each one, some silently sitting and staring; others slumped over in their chairs, some attempting to propel themselves to some distant point within the emptiness.

I swallowed and said, "As hard as I try to understand, I cannot find a reason that our loving and glorious God allows such a wretched disease to exist. I cannot fathom the reason and I will pray endlessly and respectfully to understand why. Pastor Paul is never one to be afraid to voice my concerns to God. Regardless, I sincerely thank you, Sharon, for the kind words about me, but I am just a man, nothing special. I fall short every day. Since my wife passed away, and before finally settling into life once again, well, I have made many questionable decisions."

I thought about a number of things that I did and prayed some quick thoughts for Grace, forgiveness, and acceptance.

I wiped another tear away and continued to speak, "Walter was an outstanding man and a good friend. He fought for our freedom. He was a hero in so many ways. I enjoyed his stories. They were remarkable and I love stories. Someday, somewhere, I will write his story. That is a promise. While we shared a few beers, he told me of holding many sailors' hands while they died from their wounds after some awful attack. Can you imagine? That is why I held his hand while he passed away. It was in consideration and in return for his love of his fellow brothers in arms. Besides, when Walter learned of his diagnosis and long-term prognosis, he asked me to do something for him and I promised that I would. I am very proud that I kept my promise. I had to do so. In the end, he knew me. I take great comfort in that fact, and in the fact, that, I kept my promise to him. Walter was many things, but what defined Walter the most, was that above all, Walter loved his wife forever and with honor and deep respect."

I looked at Sharon, and now Sharon had tears in her eyes too.

I continued. "Please, Walter, leaving this world and gracing Heaven is not just my loss, my dear Sharon. It is our loss. Moreover, it is this world's loss. Yet, it is Heaven's gain. Thursdays will never be the same. I think that I knew him for such a long time, perhaps, forever. Or longer."

"I think that you might be correct, Pastor Paul. Perhaps, forever. Who knows? Right?"

This time, I answered, "Right."

We both turned and looked down, The Hallway and it seemed as if The Hallway was now very different to me.

It was more than just The Hallway.

I think that in many ways, this simple hallway was really a pathway to Heaven.

THE END

Letter Two

Beloved Wife,

Rose continually tells me otherwise, but when I look back on the maze of my many careers, as a pastor, a hockey player, a bishop, a writer and all the madness in between, I always feel as if I left too much out there unaccomplished.

In reality, not much that I have done in my life has been very significant. I feel that I have failed in so many ways. All that I really have to give to you is my heart and all of my love.

My love for you is immense. It is beyond words or worldly description.

I guess that you can also include all the words in these many books that I wrote too. They are all for you, too. Somehow, someway, perhaps, these words can be my epitaph because they represent my immense love laced with words.

If those are the words that define Paul John Henson, then so be it.

Words and love woven in a tapestry of my life.

My goodness, my dear Binky, where will I find the words to convey all of my thoughts? Are they still here? Do the words hide within deep layers of emotion? I need the correct words, not just *any* words. The many adventures, they are so easy to detail. It is the words that lie within the emotions that become so difficult to find.

Perhaps they are still here.

Somewhere.

Just the other day, when I voiced my frustrations at my accomplishments, Rose made me promise to keep searching for the words that will release my thoughts, my love, and my pain. My love for her is immense, too. Her wisdom is so profound, so deep, and so all-encompassing. Her love and wisdom surround me as if they are a great cloud of glory.

I made Rose a promise. A promise to stay with the mission. Therefore, my search for the correct words continues.

After all, that epitaph needs to have some elements of validity!

Onward, I write.

Love Always,

#27

Mirror

The framed degree hung proudly on the south wall of my office. It surrounded its cloaked pride with pictures, certificates and other memorabilia of my professional life, as well as my family life and parts and pieces of my captured memories. I had my fingers poised on the keyboard to begin a story and now that my eyes caught, the Honorary Doctorate Degree presented to me many years ago by the seminary that I graduated from, I felt as if this story was going to take a different direction. A different memory surrounded me.

How silly! Often, that is all it takes in order for these stories to have life. My goodness, it was merely a glance of my eyes on a framed degree.

Rose was shopping with our daughter, Heather Sarah, and with our granddaughter, Sarah, and they would not be home for quite a long time.

Now, it was hopeless because the memories flooded my mind and I knew that this story was going to be part of the chronicles. I typed in black, bold letters, the title to the story.

"Mirror."

Off we go now.

Stirring very expensive Scotches poured neat in a glass

with your finger is not exactly the smartest nervous habit to have. I do it all the time and other than allowing me to think a bit, it is pointless and silly. When I finish stirring it, then I lick the end of my finger or rub it on my pants. Double dose of stupidity. Here I sit, in a chair, on my deck at the townhouse, gracefully sipping this Scotch, stirring it with my pointer finger and watching the sunset creep down over the horizon. A late June sunset. Stunning, oranges, reds, and even a whisk of blue and yellow highlights.

I love this deck. It is awesome. Perfect in so many ways, and it faces west. I love sunsets, and Heather Sarah and Harry knew the deck was over the top when they bought the townhouse. The deck is huge; stretching almost the entire length of the side of the townhouse, and it is one of the most amazing features of my residence. The deck is remarkable and so is the soaking tub. The tub is in my master bathroom and it is the size of a small swimming pool. I am a lucky man, but Heather Sarah tells me that I worked very hard for a long time and that I earned a little taste of luxury in my life. Maybe. I cannot help to think that the old man would take a few steps inside of this fancy joint, point at the soaking tub and proclaim his famous war cry of, "What the hell is this bullshit?"

Sure, do miss the old man.

Every single day.

Sitting next to me, on a small table, is a brand-new expensive digital SLR camera. A camera that I bought to take photographs of sunsets from the deck. Yet, as dusk approached, all I did was stir and sip Scotch, stare, think. And right now, the camera seemed to be an exorbitant waste of money.

Today's date inspired some profound thoughts. Thoughts that run through my mind while I sip my drink, sit on this deck, and while I study the sunset. It was just about one year ago, when we finished all the work we began and it all ended in a grand culmination. My goodness, how all of this crazy life whizzes by me! I sit and think about all of it and try to digest the events. God's plan never ceases to amaze me.

The townhouse is quiet these days. Ever since our daughter, Heather Sarah and our granddaughter, Sarah moved out, a year or so ago, I have lived here alone. Heather Sarah and our precious Sarah moved out when our daughter married Vance. It is a long story, but Vance is a professional ice hockey goaltender, who met our daughter when I assisted the Boston Bears with an assignment as a goaltending coach and consultant during my bereavement leave after Binky passed away. My goodness, life is so full of twists and turns. Yes, indeed, the romance of Heather Sarah and Vance Howard is a very long story!

For me, while I grow older, my life often is as it is a mirror. A mirror that reflects everything and everyone. I look at these events and see them as I saw them all years earlier, and it is a mirror of my life. I think that this mirror is another part of God's plan for me and for all of us.

Surprisingly, I am comfortable with the silence in the townhouse. Heather Sarah and Sarah lived here for almost three years and while I often miss them terribly and the daily routines we had; I find the quiet times to be lonely but acceptable.

Everyone worries about me, but I am fine. Living alone is an arrangement that I endured many years ago and I can do it now. Once more, it is a mirror.

Besides, I am never alone for too long. My family comes and goes and it seems as if everyone has a key to this place. Right now, for company, it is this sunset, this Scotch, and my constant ghosts. I lean back and watch the last teases of a sunset announce the approach of the evening. While watching, I rehash all that happened over the past few years and celebrate a magnificent memorial to a glorious man and how it influenced so many lives.

When the seminary that I attended and graduated from so many years ago, first contacted me and told me the news that the Board of Directors of the seminary had met and voted in favor of presenting to Pastor Paul John Henson, an Honorary Doctorate of Theology degree, I must say that it floored me.

The first thing that came into my mind was if Harry was still here with us, he would have asked, "Nice, but how much dough goes with it? Just a crummy piece of paper for your wall. C'mon, Paul, what's with that?"

Sure, do miss Harry.

Every single day. Every single minute. Every single second.

An old friend of mine on the Board of Directors gave me a telephone call to prepare me and a few days later, the formal letter, proclamation, and invitation arrived in the office. It came in a very fancy envelope and although she was too tough and stubborn to allow me to notice, my long-time, faithful assistant, Ms. Martha Wiggins tried unsuccessfully to hide the tears of joy that arrived in her eyes when she read the letter. The letter invited me to attend the ceremony for this year's graduating class, receive my honorary degree, and provide the keynote guest speech for the commencement ceremony. It was stunning. I honestly did not feel as if I deserved it, nor was this something that I ever expected to receive.

When the shock died down, I sat in my chair in my office and read the reasoning of the decision makers behind the bestowing of the honor.

"As an honored and respected alumnus of this seminary, the award is bestowed upon Bishop Paul John Henson, for a lifetime of contributions as a Lutheran pastor and a Lutheran bishop and his career in professional sports both as a player and a coach and mentor to young athletes. For a lifetime commitment of furthering the causes and missions of the Lutheran denominations in service to The Lord and for outstanding outreach to the communities that the church serves. As a reward for outstanding contributions as a creative and insightful writer of many important religious papers, sermons, and dissertations, and for contributions as an author of over twenty books and collections of stories dedicated to improving the lives of readers worldwide through his insight and detailing of basic human emotions within ordinary life."

Now, I needed to write a speech. I needed to make it short, too. I could hear Bishop Von Houten now, while rolling his eyes and advising, "Not too long and boring, Henson. I gotta meet Rabbi Goldberg on the golf course for a few rounds and then for a few drinks after I beat him all over the course."

I sure do miss Bishop Von Houten. He was one of a kind. I know that he will be watching and in his own special way, he will be cheering me onward.

I would do my best to convince the powers to be at seminary to address me as Pastor Paul. That bishop title is so stuffy and difficult to take.

The seminary held the commencement ceremony on a Friday evening during the last week of June and my family, friends, and even some of my old hockey teammates and coaching associates attended. The commencement committee issued me a different type of commencement cap and gown, from what they issued to the rest of my fellow "graduates" in an effort to signify my honorary status and in doing so; it was a good thing that they had a tailor come to my office to take my measurements beforehand. The tailor commented that, "He had no idea that I was six feet five and that he hoped the cap fit under all of that hair."

The presentation of the honorary degree was a very emotional and touching moment. When the president of the seminary presented the degree to me and the two of us posed for a myriad of pictures amongst blinding flashbulbs, I received a standing ovation from my fellow graduates and from the audience. Even from the stage, with the clapping and cheers from the large crowd, I could hear and then see our dear Rose sobbing as well as Martha's nose blowing amongst some tears and sobs. I knew better than ever to mention the fact that I saw and heard her crying to our dear Martha. She would deny it, anyway.

When I walked over to the podium to deliver my speech, I looked first to Heaven and crossed myself, excused myself and bowed my head while standing next to the podium on the stage, and I silently prayed. Surely, there was a grand audience in Heaven watching and cheering me onward and upward.

"I love you, Binky. Forever and beyond," I mumbled while stepping onto the podium and then I added, "yes, Bishop Von Houten and Dad, I will keep it short."

Much to the delight of all of Heaven and the crowd with slightly sweaty asses parked in the seats, I kept it short. It was late June and the joint packed the people in all the way to the rafters. Mr. Air Conditioning was doing the best that he could to offset the sweaty asses, but it was futile. My speech worked well for the present commencement class and I intertwined my own experiences here and there. It seemed to be a hit, because either I kept it short, or it actually was a good speech. I am not sure which factor was the truth, but as I watched the crowd stand and observed most of the people pulling their garments out of sweaty ass cracks, I had a good idea of which one it was.

In retrospect, it was quite an honor and certainly, it was a wonderful celebration and a forever-memorable day. After greeting what seemed as if it were most of the population of New Jersey, New York, and Connecticut, as well as meeting and greeting many of my fellow "graduates," I met up with my family and friends. First, a few warm hugs and teary-eyed kisses from Rose. She warmly embraced me, whispered how proud she was of me, how handsome I looked, and how much she loved me. Rose held me so close that I felt as if I was going to melt into her. Ever since Binky and Harry moved into Heaven, my relationship with Rose seemed to take on a different air. Little did I know what the future would bring for Pastor Paul John Henson and the lovely Rose, but that, dear reader, is indeed a different story!

The love continued with our daughter, Heather Sarah, my daughter-in-law, Blue Cloud and our son, Paul William, my sister Dottie, and her family, then all the grandchildren and my son-in-law, and then dear Martha and her family. Oh boy, it went on and on forever. It was quite the crowd! Once I worked my way through the family loving, I had mountains of friends to climb. To say that I was cared for and loved was an understatement.

Finally, the greetings ended, and the crowd broke up, and it was time to leave. The plan was to leave here and then meet back at a fancy restaurant for a reception party. But as I walked arm-in-arm with Rose and Heather Sarah, I noticed a young man standing off to the side. He was standing and watching, and I recognized the young man as the valedictorian for the graduating class. If my recollection was correct, he was not only the valedictorian for the class, but he also graduated number one in his academic ranking for the class. I only had a very brief moment to meet him in the bedlam after the ceremony, but his speech was very impressive, exceptionally well presented, and very emotional. He nodded and waved to me, and it seemed as if God spoke to my heart and that I needed to take some time to meet with him.

Of all the persons on this good Earth and maybe even in Heaven too, Rose Redmond was in tune with me more than any other person ever was. Even more in tune with me than my dear wife, Binky was. More so than even

Harry, and even more than our children were. Rose and I had been through everything together and when we were both alone in our lives, our love and our hope sustained us through the dark times. Now that we were alone again, our love and hope were going to be our greatest strength once again.

Our souls interlocked like a perfect puzzle.

Life is a mirror, and I often gazed into it.

My amazing future with Rose was yet to unfold according to God's plan, but our past was what had brought us to this point and our past is what sustained us. I am very sure that I would not be the man that I was, or even sane or alive at this point in my life, if it were not for the boundless love, endless support, and incredible spirit of Rose.

Rose followed my eyes, first to the young man standing in the corner and then to the wave of the hand of the man and the expression on his face. She felt my body posture change and my walk slow. Her intuitive nature caused Rose to pause. Heather Sarah caught on, and she leaned in and listened to the conversation as the scene unfolded.

Just above a whisper in her gentle and glorious voice, Rose spoke, "Okay, big guy, I need you to lean over because you are six-foot bazillion and I am shorter than shorter is short. Whisper in my ear and let me know what you are doing. I can tell that you are about to tell us that you will be late for the reception dinner. That duty calls."

"I am, dear Rose."

I heard Heather Sarah laugh as she listened in on how well we knew each other.

"Great," Rose moaned, with some elements of despair in her voice.

Heather Sarah then piped up, "Dear Father, this sucks more than just a little. The guest of honor is late. What do you expect us to do in order to appease the crowd? Smiles and hand puppets on the wall?"

I smiled and kissed the cheeks of Rose then our daughter and said, "Not sure, but I know that you two gorgeous women will think of something."

Heather Sarah sighed, and she handed over the car keys while telling Rose, "C'mon, Auntie Rose, Doctor Henson has a patient. I will ride with you guys."

I walked over to where the young man stood. His face lit up, and he smiled and extended his hand when he realized that his gaze and wave had initiated a response from me.

"Oh, wow, my pleasure, Bishop Henson or ah, actually, Doctor Henson."

I grasped his hand and was surprised at the strength of his hand and I matched his grip with a hard squeeze, conscious of the fact that I usually let my hand strength become too overzealous. Apparently, that was not an issue with this young man; he was tall and skinny but wiry.

I then shook my head.

Feeling the need to set this straight right away, I said, "Now, please, just call me, Pastor Paul. No doctor and no bishop title. Just, Pastor Paul works fine. I should recall your name from the ceremony and your amazing speech, but honestly, I met so many people today that your name escapes me. I apologize."

The handshake ended and the young man stepped back a little and he seemed to be collecting his thoughts. While he thought for a few seconds about what he was going to say, I studied him carefully.

As I mentioned, he was tall, not quite as tall as I was, but he was well over six feet tall. He was thin, but he had a strong and sturdy look to his frame. The young man was a good-looking man, his face was solid and chiseled and he wore his strikingly black hair long, not shoulder length like mine was, but close to my length. To keep his hair from hanging in his face, he tucked the ends of his hair behind his ears. He had full facial hair, including a thick and long beard. I generally kept my beard and facial hair trimmed quite tight and close to my face, and my beard was tough and fairly thick, but wow, this young man's beard was something that a person could live in and hide for hours. It was amazing. Yet, to me, his most striking feature was his attire. Now that commencement was over and the suits, caps, and gowns were items of the past. He wore black dungarees, black canvas sneakers and a tee shirt emblazoned with the logo and the name of a popular rock-and-roll band. It was as if I was once again looking into a mirror.

His blue eyes sparkled while he said, "I apologize, cuz, I should've remembered about always calling you, Pastor Paul. I have read all of your books and it is mentioned quite frequently in your writings." With a hint of a smile and a shake of his head, he added, "You even signed our commencement letter from the Bishop's Office as Pastor Paul. It is my great pleasure finally to meet you. I am, Mark Chapnick, and I just might be your greatest fan."

My ears caught the distinctive brogue and as I dialed it up, I knew the origin of that deep hard, accent. I knew that the next words out of my mouth would match his dialect.

We always blend.

"Nice to meet you, Mark. It is my honor that you are my biggest fan. Circling back around, your valedictorian speech was marvelous. Very well developed and certainly very well composed in theme and progression. Congratulations on your achievement today. Such a magnificent achievement." I reached into my jacket pocket, pulled out a small notepad, and waved it into the air. "Loved some of your points during that speech. I took notes. Your family must be very proud of you. I know that I was. You must have excelled in sermon composition. It was a magnificent speech."

He nodded and, almost in a low mumble, said, "Thank you. I only have my mom and an aunt and uncle left. Some cousins too. I have lost touch with my cousins as of late.

My old man is dead and so is my . . . sister. I am happy to hear you think my speech was so grand. However, I think it was lousy compared to yours. Yours blew everyone away. The guy sitting next to me was sobbing. I hid my tears because I did not want to be a mess for my speech."

"Thank you, Mark. I am sorry for the loss of your father and sister. I sense your lingering pain."

"This joint should've given you that degree, a long time ago. I am not sure what they were thinking. Their heads were in their, well, you know where. You are the best ever to graduate out of here, and besides, I like your choice of a hairstyle."

His eyes sparkled again as he gauged my tolerance to his potential use of certain words and a hint of criticism at our mutual alma mater. Then it hit me. This was more than a view in a mirror, this was part of God's plan. No other graduates had followed me and lingered to speak with me. I met them in the receiving line, exchanged well wishes and they moved on in their lives. This young man did not move on. Instead, he circled back around. Deep inside of me, I knew the feeling.

I recalled another young man who graduated so long ago from this same seminary and he had no plans and nowhere to move on, other than to his wife's arms, and into a place of faith. That young man's last name was Henson, and now, he holds this honorary degree in his hands. He did so because of many factors. I succeeded, because of hard work, a great man named Bishop Von Houten who gave me a chance, a glorious wife who never faltered in love and support of her husband's dreams, the greatest circle of loving friends that anyone could have ever had, and for sticking with God's plan. Now, I needed to find out what this was all about in the plan and in young Mr. Chapnick's life.

First, I confirmed the accent, "Are you by chance, from Paterson, New Jersey?"

"Yes, near the Clifton end. Off'a Crooks Avenue."

"I thought so. I know that accent so well."

"Yeah, man, I sound like you do. When birds of a feather flock together, our accents revert to their natural delivery. We speak as if we are polished up street thugs."

I laughed at his humor and his intelligence. His eyes were sad, but his mind was keen to the absurdities and the fun contained within everyday life.

"Yeah, I guess we do," I said, turning on a bit of northside Paterson charm. "Okay, Mark. So, what are your plans now? First in the class, a valedictorian, with great speaking skills, a handsome young man with a great smile and engaging personality. You must have knocked some congregation over with your potential. Where are you serving? Ordination? Or, do you have other plans?"

As soon as the words left my mouth and hit his ears, then I knew that I was right on target as to the sadness in his eyes. His head moved to the side, and he tried to hide his eyes. Mark nervously shuffled his canvas sneakers and in a moment of honesty, he reached out his hand and I did the same. Once more, we shook hands, and it was then that, I realized, he was bidding me goodbye.

"I really do not have any, Pastor Paul. None, but I have this cool piece of paper to hang on my wall now, saying how smart, I am. Not your problem. It is mine. Sorry. However, I did want to say hello to you, meet you, tell you how much I admire you and cross that off my list of things to do for today. I know that you need to go and meet your family and I do not want to keep you. Thank you for everything."

The handshake was over, but I still held his hand and now, I pulled him a little closer to me and when he tried to loosen the grip, I increased the strength. He was a powerful young man, but I could turn on some extra power whenever I required it.

The power did not come from my body; it came from a

much better place and I knew enough about the power and the glory to know that I could test Mark's connection to it through a special moment such as this one was. His body language and his study of my eyes told me that he was there.

"No, hey, I want to hear your story. My family is waiting for me to join up with them, but I assure you they all understand. I have a few minutes."

I let go of my grip, turned and gauged my bearings on where we were located within the facility and suggested, "I am sure that the cafeteria is closed today, but we can grab a soda or water from the vending machines and sit and chat for a bit."

"Ah yeah, sure, okay, thanks, Pastor Paul. I will show you the way."

Mark walked ahead of me. I reached out and grabbed his arm, and he stopped and looked at me, slightly puzzled as to my actions.

"Ah, Mark, unless they moved it from centuries ago when I attended here, I know the way."

He smiled and waved his hands in the air. "Of course, you do. After all, ya Doctor Henson now."

"I am, and the doctor knows best. C'mon, as my old man would have said, shake ya ass a little. I got no time for dis bullshit."

Mark laughed and picked up the pace while proclaiming, "The old man. A legend in the pages of your books and I bet in real life too. I love him, a true Paterson, New Jersey tough guy! His insight into life is brilliant."

"It was, Mark, it was and still is."

A few minutes later, we sat at a table in an otherwise empty cafeteria.

The cafeteria looked and smelled the same.

It was full of those familiar ghosts, too.

We both sipped some water from bottles and Mark told his story, "You must think that I am a copycat of Pastor

Paul, with the hair, beard, the sneakers and the rock-and-roll tee shirts, but I assure you that I was always this way. Did not play hockey or sports though, but I never fit in. I am a wayward hippie. My sister was too. We loved peace and love and we love God. We always went to church from as far back as I could recall. First Lutheran Church. It is still there."

He tapped his forehead in jest and added, "Stupid, of me. I keep forgetting ya the bishop. Of course, ya know that First Lutheran Church is still there. Mom is, and was, the driving force behind religion in our house. Dad, not so much."

I nodded and stared, signaling my understanding.

"Dad drove trucks. Mom worked in stores in downtown Paterson. Grew up in various apartments, moved around the neighborhood quite a bit. One apartment was just as dumpy as the last one was. We all grew up poor and tough, but my old neighborhood was not as rough as your side of the city, but it was no Isle of Avalon. Our parents did what they could, and I worked part time as a landscaper from high school, to community college, to college. I took student loans and accumulated debt. Still studying, as the old man would say, bullshit. Liberal arts, music courses, gonna be a rock-and-roll star or maybe, a record producer. I play the guitar and my sister, get this, she was a drummer and vocalist. You know the drill. Jam band with a Spanish kid up the street who loved my sister and played the bass guitar. We played classic rock mixed with Christian rock music, too. We were all churchgoers. Stupid dreams. Anyway, now, I had no direction in school, but I did accumulate mountains of loans that I have no chance of paying off in ten lifetimes, but during my last year in college, my world changed in many ways. First, Dad dies of a heart attack. No warning and Dad just keels over and is gone. One year from retirement and after driving trucks up and down roads for forty years, he keels over and croaks. Mom was devastated. Dad was no angel, but he was a hard worker and a good man. Not a great father, but a great provider. He had his skeletons hidden away, but I imagine we all do."

"Mark, we do. We all fall short. That is what Grace is for."

Mark nodded in acknowledgement of my statement and the power of God's Grace and then continued to tell his story, "We all went back to work full time in crummy jobs to make it all work. Mom, my aunt, my sister. Then, it grows in waves of pain and emotion, when my sister starts feeling poorly. She was about two years younger than I was and she attended community college part-time and worked full time in retail. In her junior year, it started, and it was leukemia and it sucked so badly that it tore us to pieces. We were very close and her boyfriend, Jose, I think he wanted to marry her someday, when it all sorted out in our worlds. A beautiful girl she is. Long, dark, black hair, black eyes, a great figure, and she always wore a cross around her neck and a hair band with embroidered peace signs on it in her hair. She did not last a year. A gentle and amazing soul, full of the love of God and a great vision of hope for this world. Obviously, the prayers for healing and salvation were intense and when the end came, I just could not figure out why God took her from us like that. It tore all of our hearts out and trashed our lives. Jose fell apart, and he broke down and moved away. He worshiped my sister. She was so gorgeous that she could have had any guy. They chased her all over, but she loved this skinny Spanish kid with bad skin, crooked teeth, and weird hair. True love has blinders, Pastor Paul. Jose is very smart and very cool. I miss him. No doubt, he is out there spinning in the wind somewhere. I wish that I knew where he was."

Mark remained rock solid during his story, and despite the pain, his delivery was tough and determined. Mark was an impressive young man. Battle-hardened and tested by some aspects of life's greatest challenges. I took a long sip of water from the bottle and then set it down on the table.

I pulled out the same notepad and my pen and asked, "What is your sister's name, please?"

"Patricia. The same as my mom's name."

"Your father's name?"

"James Richard."

"Thank you. Lastly, please, what is Jose's last name? What was he doing before he took off and left?"

"Torres. He attended, part time, the same community college as we all attended. He wanted to be a social worker. Help inner-city kids make it out of the pits of Hell. Jose worked as a warehouseman in some old dump over off'a Crooks Avenue. He does not work there anymore. I tried to find him and poof! Jose is gone. No one can find him. As ya know, there are quite a few people with the last name of Torres in Paterson. Every Spanish kid is a Torres. In school, when the teacher asked for Torres, ten kids raised their hands."

I loved this young man's humor tucked inside of waves of pain.

"He only has his mom here, and she has not heard from Jose in years. Tears her up too. Sucks so badly, Pastor Paul. It is terrible. I hope that he is still alive."

"Yeah, it is terrible. I admire your courage and strength. Please, I need the name of the warehouse company and Jose's last known address. I also need the address of where his mom lives. Anyway, when you get a chance, please, send it to me." I reached into my suit jacket pocket, pulled out one of my business cards, and tucked the notepad and pen away. "Here is my business card with my email address on it. Now, seminary?" I asked and picked up the water bottle and took the last long sip.

Mark nodded and began the last part of his story, "A fulfilled promise to my sister. I would never have let her down. She loved God and I do too. Patricia thought that I had the call and the gift of gab to make a great pastor, and she always told me that I was the smartest man in the world. I breezed through school, did not have to even try. Even here, in seminary, I aced it. Do not agree with all of Luther's teachings and theological conclusions but enough of them stick here and there for me to make it work. Then, when it came time to intern and meet with church leaders and congregational committees, well, you know the drill. All too well, you know the situation. I know your story. It is all too familiar. We might be kindred souls, Pastor Paul."

Mark looked at me as if I needed to fill in the parts and pieces for him.

Mirror.

Therefore, I did, "Long hair, beard, you were singing and listening to rock-and-roll songs instead of hymns. A hippie. A fish out of water, but with keen intelligence and hidden talents that no one can detect. Loads of pompous people, with an image of what a pastor should look like, act like, and display. No offers of sponsorship for ordination or calls to the pulpit. Seminary supports you on the surface, but offers little in the way of assistance or proper support. Most likely wanted your class to pick a different valedictorian. Now, you love God, but have a strong distaste for organized religion and the behind the scene politics. You have seen, observed, and felt enough of how the wheels move, and you feel that organized religion is more business than the love of God or the promotion of the Gospel. You feel as if all of this has very little to do with God, but quite a bit to do with self-promotion and filling some collection plates with a lot of jingle. How's that as a summary?"

Mark smiled and said, "As I said, they should've given that degree to you a long time ago."

"Girlfriend?" I asked.

"Nicole Grace O'Hara. Met her here. She works here in

the seminary's office. We are wildly in love, but of course, now in limbo for our future. She just left before I saw you walking down the hallway. Wavy red hair and green eyes, and an Irish spitfire heritage. Can you imagine, Pastor Paul? How gorgeous?"

"I can imagine. Yes, I can." Mark took the last sip of his water and I glanced at my watch. "Okay, let me ask you. Do you want to seek ordination? Because, I can ordain you. I need to spend some more time with you, but I sense that standing in a pulpit is not where you want to land."

Mark took the last sip of water and in an outlet of some pent-up anger; he crushed the water bottle in his hands and said, "No ordination, if it means that I will stand in front of those pompous people who turned their noses at me. No. Ordination, only if I had a mission, but right now, I have no mission. The call is dead and my sister now sees a failure."

"No, she does not see a failure. C'mon, now, Mark! Ya a Paterson guy! The old man would kick ya ass for wimping out on us. I just might too. Cut the feeling sorry for yourself bullshit."

Mark smiled and laughed, then caught his laugh and exchanged it for words, "You are correct. The old man just went nuts on me. Harry M. Redmond Junior did too. Wimping out like a punk. An ass kicking from you is not high on my happy list, Pastor Paul. Too big and too strong. You are correct. I am, sorry."

"Okay, good. Therefore, really and honestly, the world is yours. Look through the fog and the absurdities of life and see the light of hope. It is there. It is always there. It just is not so easy to see. You have to have guts, determination, and pride to see through it and to hold it in your hand. So now, suck it up and tell me, what do you want to do?"

Mark leaned back and smiled.

"Easy to answer, Pastor Paul. I have no desire to be in

pulpits or lead whacky congregations. I want to do what the three of us always wanted to do together. Either through our music or with hard work and effort, I want to help people as we are. Through the love and power and glory of God, I want to support and provide faith and love to people who grew up as we did, poor, tough and determined, and when the shit all hits the fan, show them that there is support, there are remnants of hope and there is Grace. Spread the Gospel of Hope when all that remains is despair. When all that remains, is dust. That is Patricia's dream, Jose's and my dream. Jose is Catholic, and we of course, are Lutheran, but we all are so ecumenical in our thoughts. All of this," Mark waved his hands over his head while I nodded in agreement, "this is God's entire world."

I noticed how he often referred to his sister in the present tense. I could relate.

"That is a glorious dream. Follow your dreams, Mark. Always." I then looked at my watch and asked, "What are your plans now?"

"I am going home to meet Nicole and my family. We are having a little graduation party with pizza and beer and some wine. At the apartment."

I shook my head and stood up while tossing our spent plastic bottles in the recycling trash can. Mark stood up, too.

"No, Mark, you are not having pizza at the apartment."

I recalled from long ago the great Bishop Von Houten's exact words to me while I nervously sat during a job interview, in a guest chair in his office, my office, the very office that I now sit in today. Our office.

I stole the bishop's profound words from that fateful day, "Number one in the class! Do you know how hard that is to do? Of course, you do, because you did it!"

Mark looked at me with a little puzzled look on his face at the words and after a long stare he said, "Yeah, you do, too. Cuz you did it too!"

"Exactly. Therefore, you are coming with me. We are having a big shindig at a fancy joint. Please call all of your family and Nicole and have them meet us at the restaurant. I will give you the address. Call them now while we drive there. We are going to party and celebrate like Hensons and Redmonds do. Party time!"

I put my arm around him as we walked and playfully tugged on him a little.

"Geez, Mark. C'mon, man, get with it here! Ya said that ya read the books."

"I guess now that you are a big deal, Doctor of Theology, you will not make the coffee in the morning any longer, Pastor Paul?"

"An Honorary Doctorate of Theology is really an award, rather than an earned degree. I am not sure if it earns the title of a doctor or not. Regardless, even if I could use the title, I would not use it anyway, Martha. I still will be Pastor Paul. I promise you that I will still make the coffee."

Early in the morning, on the Monday after the graduation ceremony and "festivities," I sat in the bishop's office, preparing for business as usual. However, I should know better than that, because nothing in our lives is ever usual.

My faithful and long-time assistant, Ms. Martha Wiggins, leaned back in the guest chair in front of my desk and she screwed her mouth up like a corkscrew before speaking.

"Well, Pastor Paul, I surely think after all the madness of your life and what you have accomplished, that you more than earned it. You lived it. Okay, moving on from praise for you, I still am hung-over from your party and I need coffee more than I need sex and air. Therefore, you know it is bad. I am desperate for caffeine. Until the glorious caffeine enters my bloodstream, I am in a wretched and uncontrollable downward spiral. Besides, your coffee sucks, so that might not have been a bad move for us if you decided to retire from coffee making. I figured that you would not use the doctor thingy, cuz, you hate all that fancy bullshit, but geez, after all that you have been through . . . I think that you should reconsider. Doctor Henson sounds kinda cool."

Martha was my long time, faithful and marvelous assistant. She was famous for her forthright ways, and her rather honest and "unfiltered" manner of speaking, as well as her reputation for being rather tough. We worked together for many years at Reunion Lutheran Church, and when I received the promotion to the Office of Bishop of the Northeast Lutheran District, I asked Martha to join me here in the same role. We were a team, and Martha was part of our family.

We had been together forever.

Or, maybe even longer.

Martha stood up and with a slow sigh announced, "Coffee time. I will make it today. Kinda would like the sound of my title, Ms. Martha Wiggins, Executive Assistant to Doctor Paul John Henson. Oh well, wish you had a massive and uncontrollable ego like I do."

Off Martha paddled to worship the coffee maker in the refreshment room.

I sure loved Martha Wiggins. She was one of a kind.

Back to emails and Monday madness. I was lost in work when I heard the front door to our offices open, and even while sitting in my office behind my desk, I heard Martha gasp at the sight of who had walked into the office. I looked up and I must admit it was a shock to me, too. For Martha to gasp, it takes some serious shock.

Shock, in as if winning the lottery or in meeting Jesus face-to-face type of shock. Or when Mr. Sal Zucchini Junior walks into the bishop's office early on a Monday morning.

When you are still hung over.

I stood up and waited for the scene to unfold.

"Ah, good morning, ah, ah, ah, Mr. Zucchini Junior," the normally unflappable Martha Wiggins squeaked out her feeble greeting. "Ah, it is ah, so nice to see you. Can I ah, ah, ah, help you?" Martha swallowed hard when the words left her mouth.

Standing there in our offices was the legendary Mr. Sal Zucchini Junior. He stood stoically and for the moment, silently, in front of Martha.

Remaining always the sharp dresser, Sal Junior was dressed to the hilt in an expensive, custom fitted, black suit, polished black shoes, black tie with a white shirt. He wore a black fedora and stared at Martha from behind dark sunglasses. Sal Junior was, in and around my own age, perhaps, a year or so older, but not too much older. Sal Junior was the spitting image of his dad. Bald head, a thin face with beady, deep set, piercing, black eyes. As if, Sal Senior looked into a mirror.

Mirror.

Standing right next to him were two of his faithful "sidekicks" and they were dressed the same as Sal Junior was, except there was always a telltale bulge of hidden promises of "equalizers" under the shoulders of their suit jackets. Neither of the men spoke any words. Instead, they simply stood next to Sal Junior and stared.

Sal Junior was the son of the legendary Sal Zucchini Senior. A man, who, how shall we say, conducted business in the old neighborhood. When you grow up in old New Jersey urban cities and encounter men such as Sal Zucchini Senior, you quickly learn not to ask too many questions as to the nature of their businesses. My old man taught Harry and me the ins and outs of what he graciously called, "fronts for mob joints." We learned our lessons quite well and the one thing above all that we learned is that you do not ask questions.

The stories of the many adventures of Sal Zucchini Senior and his interactions with Harry and Paul and the Henson and Redmond families will fill many pages.

Perhaps, dear reader, someday, I will find the time to do so.

Sal Senior had great respect for what we all stood for, how we acted and honestly, we all loved the man and he loved all of us. He helped us more times than we can ever imagine in so many ways, and despite the fact that we never asked what Sal Senior did for a living and he never told us, we were great friends. Sal Senior was a protector of the old neighborhood, and all it stood for, and all that it meant, and the Redmonds and Hensons were the anchors.

Sal Senior knew that fact and honored our positions and we mutually reciprocated the same honor to Sal Senior.

Sal Zucchini Senior, despite public perceptions, had a heart of gold. He passed away about five years ago after a long battle with cancer. It was my honor to have participated in his funeral service, along with the Catholic Bishop of the Paterson Diocese. A Lutheran bishop and Catholic bishop working together! The two of us walked together, leading the huge burial procession, dressed in bishop hats and garb and carrying our staffs. Catholic priests, Lutheran pastors, incense bearers, crucifers, and acolytes followed us as we led a mile-long funeral procession to the cemetery. The procession shut down the city streets of Paterson for miles! It was a written personal request from Sal Senior for me to be there and participate in the service, and there was no way that I would not have been there. You did not say, "No" to the Zucchinis! Not that I would have, anyway.

Sal Junior removed his hat and tossed it to one of his men.

"Good morning, gorgeous. You are gorgeous. Great smile and a beautiful female figure. You are a glorious woman."

Sal Junior waved his hand at Martha, as if to encompass all of her body and soul.

"I love you there, gorgeous. I would add you to the list of my, how shall we say, special friends, but they are a bit troublesome to handle now. I would shower you with diamond jewelry, tons of dough, and the best wine and da finest clothes. Ya need to call me, Sal Junior. I only allow certain people to call me, Sal Junior, and you make the cut, gorgeous. You have been with Henson forever there, gorgeous, and I trust you and love ya, too. Say there, I know, I just arrived here, but I *am* Sal Junior and I need to see Henson. Right now!"

The two sidekicks now moved for the first time as they both did not speak, but they nodded their heads to reinforce the fact that Sal Junior needed to see me right now.

Martha swooned from the arrival of Sal Junior and from the professing of his boundless love for her, and she stumbled a bit before saying, "Of course, Sal Junior. Please go right in. For you, please, no appointment is ever required."

Poor Martha held her chest, trying hard to catch her breath. She waved her hand, rather weakly, in the direction of my office. Sal Junior removed his sunglasses, folded them, and placed them in his suit jacket pocket. He then picked up Martha's hand and kissed it gently. Then he turned to one of the men and snapped his fingers. One of the men dispatched to the front door of the office for guard duty and stood there, not moving a muscle or saying a word. Sal Junior then snapped his fingers at the remaining sidekick, and the man followed his boss. Sal Junior smiled and walked into my office, and I stood and greeted him.

"Henson, Henson, Henson, how the hell r-ya? Nice to see ya." Sal Junior shook my hand as I warmly greeted him.

"Sal Junior, what a surprise and pleasure to see you. It

has been a bit of time since we visited. Please come in and sit down and tell me how you are."

The sidekick man stood next to the guest chair in front of my desk as Sal Junior settled into the chair.

"Yeah, yeah, yeah, been a while, Henson. But we are always connected."

"Yes, we are. Say, Sal Junior, I never did actually thank you for sending your Florida boys in when my daughter had a little scare there in Florida and honestly, I want you to know that. . .."

Sal Junior held his hand up, and I immediately stopped speaking. When a man such as Sal Junior asks you to stop speaking, you stop.

You come to a dead stop.

"Henson, Henson, Henson, please. What is it that Redmond Junior used to say?"

"That, I am an old lady?"

"Yes, Henson. I love you, Henson, but stop being an old lady. One call. That is all it takes, and Sal Junior and the boys are there to help. No thanks required, and no explanation needed. One call. No one messes with you and your loved ones, your friends and family."

Sal Junior breathed in deeply, leaned in closer to me, and said rather forcibly, "No. One."

The man standing guard next to Sal Junior, as well as his partner out by the front door, both emphatically nodded their heads and simultaneously patted the shoulders of their jackets to reinforce the statement.

"My father loved you, he loved Redmond Junior, and he loved your families. He used to say that we could never repay you for all you have done for all of us in the old neighborhood. You brought honor, respect, and power to all of us who called that special place home. Honor and respect, Henson. Money does not buy honor and respect. Action brings honor and respect and you are a man of action."

"Thank you, Sal Junior. You give me far too much credit, but thank you. I do not have to tell you how much I loved your father and how much he meant to Harry and to our families and me. He was a great man and I miss him every day."

Once more, the two sidekicks nodded emphatically. I thought for a second that the one man standing watch at the front door lifted his sunglasses to wipe at his eyes. But I could have been incorrect in my observation.

Sal Junior nodded, and he appeared to be in deep thought before he mumbled, "Me too, Henson. Me too."

We paused in silence for just a few minutes as if we all recalled Sal Senior in our own hearts and minds.

Sal Junior broke the silence. "Henson, say, I wanted to say how sorry I am about Redmond Junior passing so early in his great life. Talk about a great man. Redmond Junior was da best. And your wife, my goodness, Henson. What can I say? Tears my heart out. Your parents too and Redmond Senior, the Porters, and Ronzo. I loved that big guy. Ronzo. He was da best. Full of life and fun. I pray for all of you. I do."

"Thank you. And I pray for you and yours too."

"Do you realize they are all gone now, Henson? It is only you and I left from the old neighborhood. Outta all those great people, geez, man, we are the only ones left."

"I think you are correct. It is kind of amazing, but it is very true."

"Say, do you have some wine here? Henson, we need to toast to our fathers. It is just about five years now, and if I remember, your father died shortly after my father did. Alzheimer's disease, right?"

"That is correct and you are correct. The old man died about one month after your father passed. I do not have any wine, I am sorry, not even communion wine here. My portable communion kit is empty."

"What the hell, kinda bishop, are ya, Henson? Geez!

And now, I hear you are a big shot doctor guy now too!"

Suddenly a voice piped up from the front office as Martha announced, "I have something better. Top drawer in the file cabinet filed under various pains in my ass."

Martha appeared, holding a bottle of Scotch. Top shelf stuff. In her other hand, she held five shot glasses. Martha set the bottle and glasses down on my desk and with an adjustment of her huge chest and a smile, dear Martha said, "When, that nitwit, Pastor Ludlow calls complaining about some bullshit nonsense and when Henson acts like an old lady, I steal a nip or two, Sal Junior. Plus, I am the world's greatest assistant."

Sal Junior smiled and leaned back in his chair, and waved both hands in the air.

"Henson, my, what can I say? This woman is priceless. Gorgeous and priceless, and look at her gorgeous chest and curves. My goodness! You do the honors, Henson."

I nodded and poured five shots. Sal Junior waved for his men, and for Martha to gather in, and we each took a glass and raised them in a toast.

"To the old man and to my father. I am sure they are sharing laughs in Heaven. Right, Henson?"

"Right you are, Sal Junior."

"Cheers."

We tossed the drinks down, and Sal Junior waved for me to pour another round.

"One more for Redmond Junior and your wife and all the others in our families." I poured another round, and we lifted our glasses once again.

Martha shouted out, "To Redmond Junior and Mrs. Henson and all our loved ones!"

"Cheers."

Down, another shot went. Wow! It was only ten in the morning.

Sal Junior slammed his shot glass down upon my desk, smacked his lips and said, "That brings me to why I needed to see you today, Henson. I need your help. It is important . . . business. My business and your help."

Martha gathered up the bottle and glasses, and the two men returned to their posts.

Martha whispered, "Excuse me."

Sal placed his hand on Martha's arm and he gently spoke, "You stay. Put that stuff down. Please sit. You are family. Part of Henson's family so you are part of Sal Junior's family too. Sit, gorgeous."

Martha looked at me and then to Sal Junior, and I pointed to the open guest chair. Martha placed the items back on my desk, and she quickly sat down.

"Henson, ya see, I have this idea and a ton of dough. Business has been, ah, ya know, lucrative."

I prayed that Martha would not ask what type of business it was that Sal Junior participated in, but in my heart, I knew that Martha was too smart. I saw Martha study my eyes.

"My boys, who handle money, and stuff, tell me, they tell me, Sal Junior, ya got a ton of dough and ya need to, ya know, invest it some place . . . charitable. Now, I gave a bunch of dough to the Catholic parish there, ya know, Henson, c'mon help me out here."

Sal Junior snapped his fingers impatiently in the air while searching for an answer.

"You know it, cuz, you worked with those guys ovah dare. I go for confession and a special mass once a week, but I don't pay much attention to names. For obvious reasons, I have to go when no one else is dare."

"Saint Peter's Catholic Church and Father Bernard."

"Yeah, yeah, yeah, Father Bernard. I am not good with names, Henson. Thanks. They don't need more dough. They just buy fancy pictures of Jesus with the dough and new pure silver communion stuff. Instead, since it is five years since my father left us, I want a special tribute to Sal Zucchini Senior. My sister, ya see, she agrees with me, too.

We want something special to honor our father. Very special, with ties to the old neighborhood and all that he loved about it."

I leaned back in my chair and rubbed at my whiskers and while thinking I asked, "How is Michelle? It has been years since I have seen her."

Michelle Zucchini was much younger than Sal Junior was and she was a late in life reward for Mrs. Zucchini and Sal Senior. Michelle never knew the old neighborhood; she was too young to understand all of what it meant to us. Regardless, Michelle was and still is the ultimate Italian princess. Michelle was knockout gorgeous, single, and the envy of every man's desire except that she came with "extra stuff."

Michelle was always very "friendly" towards me.

"She is great. She loves you. She always had the hots for you and since youse Lutheran bishop guys can have sex and marry, she would marry you in a second and even if ya not Italian, I would bless that union."

Sal Junior leaned in close once again and said, "In a second, Henson. She loves ya, Henson."

I cleared the golf ball in my throat and mumbled, "Please, tell her that I said hello. She is a gorgeous woman."

"She don't want hello, Henson, now that you are available, she wants wild sex, and she wants to make many, many babies with you."

Martha mumbled, "Michelle needs to join the crowd."

Sal Junior looked at Martha and patted her on the back while saying, "Right? Da guy is knockout handsome and da best guy in the world but he is such an old lady."

I changed the subject in desperation as the thought of being Sal Junior's brother-in-law gave me some tingles down my spine. One wrong move with his kid sister and it is cement shoes.

"How much dough is a lot of dough, Sal Junior?"

Sal Junior leaned forward and in a low whisper, reported, "Lots and lots of dough, Henson."

"Enough, as in building a building type of dough?"

Sal Junior nodded and said, "A big-ass building, Henson. Whatcha got in mind?"

Suddenly, God's plan fully evolved in front of my eyes. I knew the last few days had a greater purpose, and I simply needed to wait this one out and let it come to me.

"About six months ago, I had a discussion with an ecumenical group working with the Paterson Diocese and St. Bartholomew's Medical Center. The group discussion centered on what the medical community could do to cope with, and support the inner-city medical needs better, and fit the changes that have happened to the city over the years. One of the suggestions that I had, involved a community outreach center for patients, families, friends who are supporting loved ones undergoing traumatic disease treatments and potentially terminal end-of-life situations."

When I mentioned end-of-life situations, Sal Junior leaned forward and whispered, "Like families and friends supporting terminal cancer patients or Alzheimer's patients nearing the end."

I nodded and continued, "Exactly. A center, to provide counseling, support, a center, housing an office staffed with experts running programs to raise charity funding for when the insurance runs out, and to assist when the costs overrun poor families. A center, providing ecumenical religious needs to all faiths and religions and love, faith and hope in the shadow of despair. My vision is a building, fully equipped for support and guidance. Educational programs of what the diseases are and what the potential treatments are all about, media and conference rooms for group therapy support, a center for hospice to work out of, an ecumenical chapel and respite rooms, a cafeteria for food and nourishment during stressful times when eating and cooking is the last thing on a loved one's mind. Honestly, we all have sat in cold, stark waiting rooms eating snacks from vending machines and drinking lousy coffee, while waiting for news on our loved ones to arrive. It is not fun."

Martha, Sal Junior, and his two men all nodded their head in agreement. I know that commenting on my lousy coffee was on the tip of Martha's tongue, but she resisted the urge to tease me.

"Sal Junior, I feel that a loving and caring environment for support during those times would be a huge boost to persons who, at a very critical juncture in their lives, need hope, love, and support in order to cope with what they are dealing with in their lives. I foresee a community center, working in conjunction with a renowned medical center for supporting inner-city families and the downtrodden, while families stay and support their loved ones during operations or treatments. I envision this world-class building built on the campus of the medical center's campus."

I leaned back in my chair and waved my hands in the air as if I was duplicating a theater marquee sign and proudly stated, "I see, the Sal Zucchini Senior, Community Center for Outreach and Support. I see, a huge oil portrait of your father hanging in the lobby and underneath the portrait in glorious words, it states, 'In loving memory of Mr. Sal Zucchini Senior for his dedication, tireless support, and love for the residents of his beloved Paterson, New Jersey."'

I was lost in the passion of the moment and when I finished my long speech and delivery of my vision; I studied Sal Junior's eyes. Martha did too. The two sidekicks stood silent, but I am sure underneath their glasses they also waited for his reaction. Sal Junior stared at me, his dark and beady eyes not moving at all, and I rather intensely stared at the eyes of Sal Junior.

Finally, Sal Junior leaned in and asked, "Henson, this here committee—what did they think of your idea?"

"They loved it but everyone thought it would take years and years to raise that kind of money to build such a center. It would cost a ton of dough even with the St. Bartholomew's Medical Center able to donate the land located right next to the hospital. They own tons of land that are now just vacant lots in the inner city. They knock down those old buildings right and left these days."

"Vacant land that the diocese owns, huh, Henson?"

"Yes."

Sal Junior turned to Martha, and his face broke into a smile. In all my years of knowing both Sal Junior and his father, I think I saw them smile about five times.

Maybe six.

Michelle smiled all the time, flipped her hair, and pointed her giant chest at me.

She does not count.

"You see, gorgeous. This is why this man is a genius."

The two men emphatically nodded once again.

"It would be the ultimate honor for our father. Cancer took him from us. He would want this for the city. The people of Paterson need this."

The two men, Martha and I, all emphatically nodded. Tears began to form in the eyes of Sal Zucchini Junior, and in Martha's eyes, and I reached in my desk drawer and pulled out a box of tissues. Sal Junior offered the tissues to Martha. She pulled one out, and dabbed at her eyes, Sal Junior took one and dabbed at his eyes. When they finished, I took the box of tissues and walked over to the first man, he took one and dabbed at his eyes underneath his sunglasses, and I handed the box to his buddy, who nodded, took one and he did the same. I returned to my desk and sat down.

Sal Junior leaned back and looked at his sidekicks and snapped his fingers while instructing, "Not a word about the tissues! Right?"

The two men emphatically nodded once again.

Assured that his weepy-eyed moment was forever secret, Sal Junior shifted gears and said, "I love this, Henson! Let's do it. The dough is yours! I want your daughter to run this all. We will set up a not-for-profit corporation in Sal Senior's memory and name it after him. Your daughter is a great attorney . . . she is da best! She does all this legal work for Redmond's many charities, your father-in-law's stuff, Rabbi Goldberg's and the old bishop's charities. Right?"

"She does, yes, she does. That is her specialty. Legal support for charities."

Sal Junior waved his hand in the air and said, "Done deal. I trust only Henson and Henson's daughter with this. I have trust issues. Remind me, Henson. Her name? I am bad with names, Henson."

"Heather Sarah."

Sal Junior sat back in his chair and he smiled again.

Seven times.

It was a smiling type of day.

"A gorgeous name. She is gorgeous, like her mother. Gorgeous. We will set up a Board of Directors. Henson's daughter runs it, Henson you are on it, and Redmond Junior's widow, is on the board. What is her name? I am not good with names. She is gorgeous too."

"Rose."

"Yes, Rose. Italian too. That woman makes a man's soul shatter and break out in cold sweats because she is so gorgeous."

The two men emphatically nodded once again. I surmised that they saw or knew of the lovely Rose.

Sal Junior put his arm around Martha and proudly said, "And gorgeous here is on the board."

Martha seemed stunned and when she recovered Martha said, "Oh my. Me? Really?"

"Sure, gorgeous, we need someone to tell Henson when he is acting like an old lady and make the coffee because Henson sucks at making coffee."

"You are correct, Sal Junior."

"Of course, I am correct, gorgeous. I am Sal Junior."

The two men emphatically nodded once again.

Sal Junior then sat and thought for a few moments and after thinking he said, "One more board member. I want that whacked out old hockey player buddy of yours and Redmond Junior's on the board. The guy who became a minister. Help me, Henson, with his name. I am not good with names. Crazy, maniac, tough guy. Would've beaten the hell outta his own grandmother over a hockey puck. Whack job guy with a heart of gold."

The two men emphatically nodded once again.

"Pastor James T. O'Malley."

Sal Junior pounded my desk and yelled, "That's da guy! Love that guy. We need an enforcer on the board."

"I can assure you that Jim will be thrilled at the honor of serving."

"Great! Let's do this, Henson. Have your daughter contact my legal boys and my construction boys too. My construction boys will build this place, ya know, Henson."

"Yes, of course."

"Good."

I was curious, so I asked, "And what about you, Sal Junior?"

Immediately, he answered, "No, Sal Junior does not go out in public very often. I am sure that you understand, Henson. I need to keep public appearances to a minimum."

The two men emphatically nodded once again.

"Yes, of course. I understand, Sal Junior."

Now it was time to mention one last item. The reason that I truly believe this all evolved as it did so, with the timing of the moment.

"Sal Junior, we will need a director for the center. We

need someone dedicated to the mission, a person who understands the inner city and all the things that this center will be about to honor your father and his legacy. I think it is advantageous to bring this person on right away. From the start, so their input is part of the vision, the construction, the planning."

Sal Junior nodded his head, and anxiously waved his hands in the air, and said, "I agree. Go on, Henson. No old lady bullshit, ya gotta get to da point. Sal Junior is a busy guy. Ya got someone in mind?"

"I do. A young man who graduated seminary this past weekend. My seminary, where they awarded me the honorary doctorate. He is passionate and very intelligent. In fact, he graduated number one in his class, and he does not want to serve as a pastor in the pulpit or take a parish assignment to lead a congregation. He wants to do social work in the inner city."

"Okay, yeah, sounds nice. I like the way this sounds and the idea, but if ya think. . .."

I now had the courage to interrupt Sal Junior's end of the conversation. Sal Junior was not used to interruptions. The interruption took courage, and it caused Martha, the two men, and Sal Junior, some pause and startled everyone. Sal Junior's eyes grew wide at the boldness of my interruption, but softened when he realized why I did so.

"Sal Junior, he is a Paterson kid. Grew up in the city. Crooks Avenue area. Rough and tough, poor kid. He has long hair and a beard, as I do. His old man was a truck driver. He died suddenly at work of a heart attack, and his sister, when she was barely twenty years old . . . she died of cancer. Specifically, of leukemia."

Sal Junior leaned in and without changing his facial expression, Sal Junior asked, "Leukemia, huh? Like my father had. Do you trust him, Henson?"

"I do, yes, I do. He has honest eyes. I feel as if God spoke to my heart, and this is all part of God's plan."

"Then go get him, Henson. He is the first employee."

"Do you want to meet him first?"

"Not if you say, he is the man. Hell, he is a Paterson kid! Henson, go get his ass and tell him that Sal Junior wants him to be part of the team and Sal Zucchini Junior stands behind everything he sells, says, and does."

"Sal Junior, he has lots of student loan debt and he might not be able to work for a lower wage."

"Bullshit, we pay top dollar! Tell ya daughter that we pay top dollar. Tell her, ah, what is her name, Henson? I am bad with names."

"Heather Sarah."

"Yeah, Heather Sarah. Tell 'em all that we will write a check and pay that all off as part of his employment contract. We saddle these young people with mortgages without houses. Bad scene. What else, Henson?"

I reached into my desk drawer and pulled out a piece of paper written with Jose's information, his last known employment and address.

I handed it to Sal Junior, who studied it, and when he looked up, I said, "I need to find this guy."

Sal Junior nodded, snapped his fingers and immediately the man next to Sal Junior snatched the paper and nodded when Sal Junior said, "Find this guy. Now!"

Sal Junior looked at me and asked, "Henson, do you want him, ah, how shall we say, persuaded to do something, or do you need him to ah, well, disappear?"

I watched as the one man tapped his shoulder to confirm the presence of the "equalizer."

"No, no, no, please, just find him for me. He is a good guy and he will be part of the team."

Sal Junior nodded, and the two men nodded in agreement too.

"Done deal, Henson. We will have the information on dis guy to gorgeous here by tomorrow afternoon. We are, how shall we say, *good* at finding people. Now, let's have another toast. Gorgeous, ya pour 'em this time. Henson is an old lady, and he pours 'em too short. Did anyone ever tell ya that ya got a great smile and a fantastic chest?"

We downed another round, then we bid goodbye to Sal Junior, and his men. Martha swooned when Sal Junior kissed her hand again and emphasized that she was gorgeous. When they finally left, Martha came into my office, flopped in the guest chair and sighed.

"It is only noon, and I am half in the bag from toasts, exhausted and hungry as hell. Doctor Henson, do you have a diagnosis and prescription?"

"I do. You are suffering from the effects of Zuchinnitis and God's glorious plan. I prescribe that we head for The Elusive Lion Pub, eat lunch, and drink away the rest of the day. We can have a working lunch and afternoon, because, once I call, Heather Sarah, and tell her about this unbelievable morning, then we all will have a ton of work to do."

"Doctor Henson, I love your style. How is your bedside manner? Sorry. That might have been inappropriate as an employee to a boss type of comment. On the one to ten, Martha Scale of Various Inappropriate Comments to my unfairly handsome and sexy boss that I have made over these many, many years that one might be a seven. On the other hand, maybe an eight. In a vain attempt at self-defense, I invoke a Sal Zucchini Junior clause. Too many toasts and comments about how gorgeous I am. Stirred up my hormones. As I said, I had way too many toasts, but what the hell, a woman can dream. Can't she?"

I sure loved Martha Wiggins.

About two long years or thereabouts, later after that fateful meeting in the office, the dream became a reality.

The glorious Sal Zucchini Senior Community Center for Outreach and Support Building stood in front of us.

It was magnificent.

And so was the oil portrait of Sal Zucchini Senior hanging in the lobby.

Hard work, yes, but it was worth it and the contribution that this facility and the persons working inside of it will make, will be beyond glorious to the gritty, but, the wonderful city of Paterson, New Jersey.

I had to think that Sal Zucchini Senior was very proud of all of us.

The entire Board of Directors team of the Sal Zucchini Senior Community Center Foundation, proudly stood in front of the center, along with the new Director of Operations, Pastor Mark Chapnick, his wife, Mrs. Nicole Grace O'Hara Chapnick and the Assistant Director of Operations, Mr. Jose Torres. We had just opened the center in a formal ribbon-cutting center and the media just left. The ceremony was over and now; the keys were Pastor Mark's and it was time to get to work.

As the old man would say, "Time to shake ya ass and get to work."

While we stood in front of the center, we all turned and watched as two big, black Galaxy 4000 vehicles with blacked-out windows came roaring down the driveway in front of the center. We watched in awe as the two cars pulled into the driveway and the first car screeched to a halt. Right behind it, the other big, black Galaxy 4000 with blacked-out windows pulled up and stopped behind the first car. We all turned, looked, and our mouths dropped open, when a man dressed in an impeccable black suit, white shirt and a black tie, wearing black sunglasses and a stoic expression, jumped out of the front door of the first car, and stood next to the back door of the Galaxy 4000!

He looked at Martha and me from behind his dark glasses and nodded.

Martha leaned in and whispered, "Pastor Paul . . . that is one of the men, who came with Sal Junior to the office on that day when we met."

I nodded in agreement.

Six more of Sal Junior's men jumped out of the doors of the second Galaxy 4000 and surrounded the first car. They all were dressed in dark suits with their usual sunglasses on, and they scanned the entire area while they were watching everything. In unison, the entire team of henchmen patted their suit jackets in the shoulder areas.

Once the area was "secure," the first man, or what we presumed to be the, "head henchman" nodded and the security team opened the rear doors to the vehicle. On the driver's side, Sal Zucchini Junior stepped out, and on the passenger's side, Michelle Zucchini stepped out. Sal Junior wore his usual black suit, dark sunglasses, and his trademark fedora and Michelle; well, she looked gorgeous in a skin-tight black dress, with a plunging neckline, and black high heels.

Her perfume could knock a buzzard off of roadkill.

Her breasts extended to the next cross street.

Sal Junior nodded to me, while the team of black suited henchmen surrounded them, and the two Zucchinis made their way over to where we all stood in awe. Sal Junior warmly greeted me and after shaking my hand, he leaned in and kissed both of my cheeks in a traditional, old-world greeting.

"Henson, I love you. Great job! This is one of the proudest moments in my life. I knew that you would pull it off, no doubt in my mind."

Michelle was not so gentle or traditional. She cut right to the chase. While in, and amongst frowns from Rose, Martha, my daughter-in-law, and my daughter, she waltzed up to me, swaying her glorious hips, bouncing her enormous breasts, and she ignored my extended hand and instead, grabbed my face, pulled me down to her level and kissed me on my lips, long, deep and hard.

"Henson, you are a magnificent specimen of manhood. I would wear you out, night and day. I would only let you come up for air. A few short breaths so we can make love some more. Over and over. All day. All night. Call me, please. Call me tomorrow and marry me next week. Oh yes, thank you for Daddy's building."

I staggered back from the combination of the perfume and the power of the kiss and mumbled, "You are welcome. And thank you for the greeting. Nice to see you again, Michelle."

Heather Sarah steadied me and whispered to me, "Easy, dear Father. Don't faint and don't even go there. She will kill you in one night. Her mountainous breasts will suffocate you."

"Henson, introduce me to the team here. I know your daughter, and gorgeous here, but I am not good with names."

"Sure, Sal Junior, this is Heather Sarah, and this is my daughter-in-law. . .."

When we reached the end of the line, I introduced Director of Operations, Pastor Mark Chapnick, his wife, Mrs. Nicole Grace O'Hara Chapnick, and the Assistant Director of Operations, Mr. Jose Torres. Mrs. Chapnick and the two men nervously shook Sal Junior's hand and professionally greeted Michelle.

Mark spoke, "It is such a great and immense pleasure to meet you, sir. Thank you, Mr. Zucchini Junior, for this opportunity and all that you have done for Jose and for my wife and for me. I promise you that we will do a great job and honor your father and all that he stood for."

Sal Junior stood back and asked, "Pastor? I thought you were not ordained?"

"I decided that the job required a pastor title to do proper honor to the mission, so I asked Pastor Paul to ordain me. This way, I can make the commitment to the center and to God."

Sal Junior stepped back and looked puzzled.

"Who ordained you?"

"Ah, Pastor Paul, sir."

Martha, knowing Sal Junior well enough now, stepped over and whispered, "Henson."

Sal nodded and whispered, "Got it. I am not good with names. I love you, gorgeous. You da best. Great chest too." Sal Junior cleared his throat and faked his way through the rest of the scene.

"Yeah, yeah, yeah, Pastor, ah, ah, Henson. Look, kid, ya a good-looking kid. Ya remind me of Henson. Ya like as if we are looking in a mirror at Henson. Ya a Paterson kid, right?"

"I am, yes sir, so is Jose."

Sal Junior nodded and smiled.

Eight times.

Sal Junior began a long speech, "Good. Your wife is gorgeous. To the moon, gorgeous. Guard her honor and love forever. It is important to have a faithful companion in life. It gets rough at times. I like ya, kid. Henson is right cuz ya got honest eyes. Do us proud, Chapnick. That name on the front of that building means everything to us. Our father loved this city with all his heart and soul. He always wanted the people of this city to have a chance. No matter, what language they spoke, or what color their skin was, or which way they addressed, God. He only wanted a fair shake for everyone. Do us proud. I am watching, along with my father and most importantly, Henson is watching."

Sal junior turned around and pointed at me.

He then continued, "The man is a direct conduit to God. Believe me when I say that he is. He is what a man of God is all about and our father, my sister, and I love him. Like I said, ya gotta do us proud. Do Paterson proud and help the people who need it the most. I swear that the mission can never fail, and remember, Chapnick, that Sal Zucchini Junior stands behind everything that he sells, says, and does. Be cool, Chapnick and, ah . . . other guy."

Sal Junior, play punched Mark and then Jose in the arm, he took Mrs. Chapnick's hand and gently kissed it, nodded his head, tipped his hat and stuck his arm out for his sister to lock her arm inside his, while they made their way back to the vehicles. The henchmen surrounded them in great waves of protection.

The two Zucchinis stopped by me and Sal Junior said, "Henson, I meant it when I said that we love you. You are a great man, Henson, A really, really, great man. You bring a lot of joy and happiness to people's lives, who otherwise, would have very little, and that is very important. We can never repay you for what you have done. Ever. Thank you. Be cool, Henson."

His words caused a shiver or two up and down my spine. I had heard Sal Senior say very similar words many years ago.

Michelle blew me a kiss, mouthed that she loved me and for me to call her, and with an opening of the doors, a start of an engine, and a peel of rubber—they were gone. I had witnessed a very similar exit such as this one was many times in the past. However, what did Sal Junior say?

Something about a mirror?

The Scotch is gone and so is the sun. It was a glorious sunset and despite the fact that the camera remained idle at my side; I felt as if I captured the glorious colors in my mind. It was worth it. I just have to stop stirring my Scotch with my finger. That was a bad habit. Pastor Mark and Jose do an outstanding job at the Sal Zucchini Senior Community Center, and no doubt, God's work and plan are very apparent and strong there. Pastor Mark is a very gifted man, and he has carried out the mission with honor and diligence.

Mark's sister is very proud of them.

I only occasionally hear from Sal Junior these days.

It does not matter; it is just as Sal Junior always said, "We are always connected."

The old neighborhood will never die. It was too special ever to die. Through the grapevine, I heard that Michelle gave up on chasing me and that she is now married.

Thank goodness! Good luck to that chap. He had better not make any missteps with Sal Junior's precious kid sister. Cement shoes fit everyone.

Life is often a mirror and on this go around it was worth it to stare into the mirror. You never know what image God will send back to you! I picked my glass up and the camera, too. I was a little weary.

Tomorrow is another day and another opportunity to stare into a mirror. Hold on, Pastor Paul, or ah, Doctor Henson, because you never know what will be looking back at you this time.

The warm embrace of Rose hugging me around my neck shook me back to reality. She had returned from her shopping trip, and her timing was perfect. This story was in the book.

"Hey, my love, whatcha working on? Is it more of your chronicles? My goodness, Paul! I would ask you the subject of your latest masterpiece but I know better. You never clue me in on any details of stories in progress and I am fine with that. I love to read the finished work and be surprised. So, another one in the works, but I have to ask you, Paul, will they ever end?"

That was a very good question.

"Yes, more chronicles and no, I am not sure when and if

they will ever end. I began early this morning with an idea and totally and completely shifted gears into a different direction."

Rose let go of me and walked around to the front of the desk and she sat on the edge of the desk and stared at me. My goodness, my memory of Sal Junior's comment on that day a few years ago, about the gorgeous Rose Henson was so correct. This woman makes a man's soul shatter and break out in cold sweats because she is so gorgeous.

Rose must have caught my eyes staring at her because she smiled and asked, "What? You have a funny look on your face."

"No, funny look, I just recalled something that I wrote about how gorgeous you are. I love you, Rose."

"You wrote about how gorgeous I am? Well, thank you. I love you too, Paul. All of my heart and soul. Are you finished writing for today? I think it is time for you to take a break. My goodness, you have been at it for over twelve hours. You work harder now that you are supposedly retired than you ever did and you worked like a mad demon at those jobs too. Come along now and take a break. I will show you the slinky sleepwear that I bought today and we can have dinner, some drinks, and relax. Maybe we can find an old movie to watch. Do you want to do that?"

"I do! Sounds great. Maybe we can find one of those old gangster movies, you know, the ones with a smooth-talking mobster guy who wears a black fedora and who is really not a bad guy after all. Maybe, he has a sister who is a knockout too, and the sister falls for the policeman, trying to catch them. I wanna watch a really old one, black and white, with crackles in the sound."

Rose looked at me with a hint of a smile and a shake of her gorgeous head.

"I guess, I am sure we will find something to watch. If not, we can neck and have throwback teenage foreplay on the couch. Somehow, I think that I know some of the characters in the story you wrote today. Anyway, c'mon, Hemingway, yes, let's do it and then later on, well, you know."

"I love the later on part combined with the new slinky sleepwear. And no comment on any of my characters."

I saved the file and nodded my head. I was done, and with an invitation like that one, I knew where tonight was leading. It was not about sunsets or cameras or looking in a mirror. It was actually about the same subject that my story was about today. Hidden underneath all the characters, the memories, and the ghosts, the story is really about love. A family's love for their father and his love for them. A metaphor for God's love for us and our love for God.

Sometimes when it all boils down that is actually what God's plan entails.

A huge dose of love.

THE END

Letter Three

Beloved Wife,

Perhaps it is my imagination, but I often swear that, when I am sitting at my desk and writing, I hear your footsteps in the hallway outside my office. This is even when there are no outside influences of alcohol involved. Ha! I swear, dear Binky! I mentioned it to Rose, and she does not seem to think that it is my imagination. Rose says that it makes sense that you are so close to us.

Why not? Maybe Harry is here too. It makes sense, but I really do not know. I often feel as though his touch is on my shoulder and I can hear that special laugh of his in my ear.

All the adventures tend to jam up into one another and they run around in my mind in a maze of confusion. I try hard to sort them all out and decide which ones to record. The memories are so clear and they come along in giant waves crashing into my head at the most unusual times. Some are fun and some tear me apart. I wish that I could just hear your soft voice one more time, hear your laugh, and watch you walk across the kitchen floor of the parsonage at Reunion Lutheran Church. On the other hand, to see you waving at me while I step off the train, while you sit in my faithful, old jeep in the parking lot at the train station in Great Falls. Your smile, breaking my exhaustion after a long day at the seminary in the city. Yes, indeed, one more time. But then, I would need so much more.

Dear Binky, do you think that these adventures will ever stop running through my mind? Each memory seems to spawn another one! Endless adventures in crashing waves, and often when I hear your footsteps in the hallway, I think that you will poke your head around the corner of the door and smile at me while seeing what I am doing. However, every time I look up, the hallway is empty, and the doorway is void of your lovely face.

What a great mystery this thing we all call life is! I stop and recall our journey through the pain, the amazing joy, and the spectacular happiness. It is then, in the quiet stillness of a late Saturday evening, when Rose is fast asleep and my Scotch glass is empty, it is then that I hear the voices call, and the ghosts speaking to me, and I realize that I have so much more to write about, dear Binky. Write about you, of me, of Harry and of Rose and all our friends and family and of all we shared, now and forever.

All we shared.

When you are lost and then found again, it is a glorious feeling, and the words that I place on paper continue to restore my soul one piece at a time. In the back of my mind, I wonder what will happen when I run out of words. Will that mean the stories and adventures are finally complete?

Perhaps.

Until then, I will write on and listen very carefully for Harry's laugh and your footsteps in the hallway.

I promise that I will listen very, very carefully.

Love Always,

#27

The Awakening

When I assumed the position of Bishop for the Northeast District of our Lutheran synod, I always found it to be an ironic twist of fate that a traditional English pub was located within walking distance of my new office. Perhaps it harkened back to my family's heritage, or in my case, I chose to believe it was divine intervention on my behalf. In retrospect, for this somewhat reluctant Lutheran pastor and even more so a huge doubter of my qualifications to be a Lutheran bishop, the fact that "The Elusive Lion Public House" was located smack-dab in the center of the downtown area of Newark, New Jersey was, a sign from God that God wanted to keep me afloat.

In more ways than one.

Paul John Henson will take all the help and inspiration that he can receive

I not only enjoyed a few beers and food in the pub, but I also conducted business there. The relaxed atmosphere can be very conducive to productivity and at times can be much better than struggling through meetings in a stuffy office in a high rise. If I was anything, it *was* unconventional, and certainly uncategorized. Generally, the last profession that a person who met me for the first time would think that I sought my employment in would be for me to serve as a Lutheran clergyman. Long hair, beard, rock-and-roll tee shirts and black canvas sneakers, a former professional ice hockey player, turned Lutheran clergyman, eventually promoted to the position of the bishop and responsible for leading congregations and pastors from New Jersey to Connecticut, to New York and beyond. . ..

Certainly, it was no time to change now. And besides, my loyal and amazing wife of so many years, Binky Hobnobber Henson used to encourage me to stay exactly as I was.

I think that I will. Opinions never swayed me, then or now.

"No sense in changing a winning formula," remained my wife's advice and in many ways, her longtime battle cry. I missed Binky, more than words can ever convey. Her tragic death left a hole in my heart and in my soul. With God's assistance, I crawled out of the hole and carried on with my life.

Dear reader, another story and another time and place for in the future.

It was a Friday afternoon in late August, and after many years serving as the bishop and before this position as a pastor, I worked my share of long days, weekends and Fridays. Most pastors took Fridays off since they had to work on Sundays, but I never practiced the Friday leisure day until much later in my career. I think that I paid the price for that foolishness because I missed too much precious time with my wife and children.

Now that my wife was a saint in Heaven and the children had long since grown and ventured out on their own, I longed for that missing time until it made my heart ache with the thoughts of it. Even if I could never recapture all that lost time, and even if I no longer preached a sermon in a pulpit every Sunday, I came around to some of my senses and compromised by taking Friday afternoons off during the summer.

My long-time, faithful assistant Martha Wiggins breathed a long sigh of relief when I told her of my plans; of course, Martha wanted me to take every Friday off during the year, but to this old dog that was a new trick that I just could not learn.

Before wrapping up for the day, I changed out of my black suit and white collar, and dressed in my favorite leisure garb of choice with my worn black canvas sneakers, a tee shirt emblazoned with the logo and name of my favorite rock-and-roll band and black dungarees. My long hair, originally blonde with licks of red highlights, now had some edges of gray contained within, and the whiskers on my face sported some white and gray hairs, too. Not too many, considering my age, but there is little doubt that between my attire and my choice of hair styles that I looked, as if I was just an old leftover hippie from a bygone era.

Now, the afternoon of leisure found me sitting on my favorite bar stool at my favorite pub, while enjoying an early supper of some English patsy. Keeping with my own traditions, I dutifully washed it down with my favorite beer, which was the famous New Jersey brew known as "Big Boulder." Hardly, a craft beer or the finest beer selection but as I mentioned, the old dog and new tricks aspect of my personality.

"Be right back to chat a bit, Pastor Paul. You look stunning today as usual and my heart is all a flutter at the sight of you. It has been a crazy, but lucrative afternoon."

Out of the corner of my eyes, I saw the man who was sitting next to me swing his head around in surprise and I noticed his frown and his eyes narrow in a careful study of the scene in front of him. It seemed as if he noticed when the long-time bartender of "The Elusive Lion Public House" and my close friend, Ms. Jennifer Hollingsworth, addressed me as "Pastor Paul." His eyes widened while she leaned in and gave me a gentle peck of a kiss on my lips, along with a coy wink.

The man was sitting on a stool just a few short feet or so away from mine. Technically, it was the next stool to my immediate left, but the curve of the bar extended the distance. Still, it was within easy earshot, and Jennifer's words caught his ear and caused him some pause while he carefully studied me. I saw him abruptly place his drink glass on the bar counter and I carefully watched him out of the corner of my eyes. His eyes looked me up and down. He continued to lean our way as the lovely, and captivating Jennifer leaned close to me for some discussion. A leftover habit of mine from my hockey goaltending days was always to watch a shooter's eyes for a clue as to where the shooter intended to shoot the puck. A habit that carried over to my new profession, too. The man sitting next to me was sipping a drink and poking at his sandwich, and until Jennifer and my mutual interactions and exchange of words, I had not even noticed him sitting there. The bar had been busy and now that the lunch crowd waned, Jennifer had some more time to slide over to me and chat for a bit. For a brief moment, I thought the man was studying the glorious beauty of Jennifer Hollingsworth as she leaned in close to me. But after a few quicker glances, I realized that I was indeed, the subject of his careful study. After a few seconds of his pause, the man picked his drink back up, and he sipped it. I could tell that he was still interested in our conversation and presence.

I had known Jennifer for more years than I could even measure. Martha and I would often have lunch and dinner together at "The Elusive Lion" and Jennifer was always our server and honestly, our friend. In keeping with public house traditions, Martha and Pastor Paul even had a small, brass plaque mounted in our honor with our names stamped on it and happily screwed into the wood clapboards above our favorite table.

After Binky passed, Jennifer was more than kind. And for a short period of time, I sensed that Jennifer had some romantic hopes that our relationship might change from friendship to something that was quite different from merely a close friendship. We went to dinner together a number of times, a fancy restaurant, Jennifer all dressed out to the hilt, looking captivating and quite stunning. Yet, I made it clear that I wanted only to remain friends. I valued her friendship and her insight into life and sincerely conveyed my feelings to Jennifer.

There was very little doubt that Jennifer seemed disappointed, but she understood and never pressed me to steer our friendship into anything other than what it was and is. I never gave her any false indications, nor did I ever imply that we were anything but very good friends. For now, I remained far short of seeking any new romantic relationships, and if, and when, I did feel anything, then I knew that it would be part of God's plan to steer me where I was supposed to go in my life. While Jennifer was gorgeous and had a kind soul, as well as an engaging personality, I had no current romantic inclinations toward Jennifer. She was, and I hoped that she always would be, a very good friend. If God's plan was for our relationship to be something different, then I had confidence that the plan would all evolve in good time. Until then, I remained within my own little world, albeit as strange as I composed it to be, but I kept within my own thoughts and certainly remained a victim of my own visions.

Today, since I was alone, I sat on my favorite stool at the bar. No plaque, but it was my favorite.

"Sorry, I have been slammed here," Jennifer said as she returned to my position at the bar. She leaned over the counter, gently took the pen from my hand, and placed it down next to the pad that I was doodling on and then she continued, "Whatever you are working on there in noting your endless thoughts, please take a little break and tell me how you are. I have not seen you since last Friday and I miss your face when you are not around more often."

I surrendered the pen to Jennifer with a smile on my face and I mumbled, "Okay. That is fair enough. No writing for a few minutes. I was passing the time until you could shake free. I saw how busy you were."

Jennifer smiled and coyly asked, "And, and, and, what else?"

I feigned that I was unaware of the answer to her question, and when she put her hands on her hips and frowned a bit at me, I blurted out, "Oh, yes! I missed you too."

"That is better. Now, what is going on in your world?"

"Everything is okay. You know, the end of the summer looms, churches are quiet, and people are on vacation. Martha is planning her Jersey shore getaway. I am okay, not great, but ok." Jennifer twirled the pen in her fingers. It looked as if she wanted to say something, but she passed on her initial statement and instead held the pen steady and studied my eyes.

Jennifer knew me quite well.

We had known each other for quite a bit of time, and since Binky passed, I was transparent to my friends and family.

"Bad week, huh?"

"Yes, it is. Many ghosts. How about you?"

"I dunno, Pastor Paul. Too busy to worry much about it. The bar scene has been hopping, glad we are reaching the quiet hours. It has been so stiflingly hot this summer that everyone escapes to enjoy lunch here. I am happy for the money, but long for these quiet hours, after the lunch crowd and before the dinner hour. What you always call, supper."

I nodded and watched as Jennifer's eyes darted away from me to a patron, leaving the bar. She had to go back to work. Jennifer was a pro and there was not too much, which she missed.

"Here is your pen back. Keep purging pain on that paper until I return. Maybe, we should plan on dinner tonight, if you need to talk and do not want to be alone. I get off at six. Unless . . . you had other plans."

I nodded, but did not answer her as she first checked on the man next to me, and then convinced that he was okay, on his meal and his drink, off she darted to tend to the other end of the bar. I took a long sip of my beer, dashed the last few forkfuls of my supper away in hopes of finishing eating, to allow some more time to chat with Jennifer, and then pushed the empty plate away.

I held the pen poised over the paper, when I heard the man next to me clear his throat and ask, "Did I hear the bartender address, you as, Pastor Paul?"

I turned and looked his way while confessing to my own mind that until Jennifer turned and looked at him and now that he spoke that, I had even forgotten his presence there. Jennifer's soft voice and her amazing beauty could do that to a man.

The man took a sip of his drink and I studied him for a brief moment or two. I would guess him to be middle age and except for some thin locks of hair swirling on top of his head and a tuft or two of black hair layered above each of his ears, he was mostly bald, had a thin face, and he wore thick eyeglasses. He carefully studied me and while his eyes followed me, I carefully noticed his attire. He was dressed in a black suit, white shirt, and a black tie with silver stripes in a vertical pattern. The bulge of the shirt told of the girth of his belly, and his belt disappeared within the rolls of the shirt.

"Ah yes, indeed. Hello. Good afternoon. How are you?" I smiled, and I continued, "yes, Pastor Paul John Henson. I am a Lutheran pastor."

The man instantly frowned, and I knew this was going to be one of *those* kinds of interactions. I faced way too many of them over the years. Long hair, beard, my attire, drinking beer in a pub; many strikes against me in his eyes.

Ugh. Not too sure I was up for this one. Just as I had told Jennifer, this had been a bad week. For a brief moment, since my beer was almost gone and my meal was finished, I thought that booking out of here and circling back with Jennifer later on would be the best option, but something inside of me told me to stay put.

"I am surprised to see a Lutheran pastor drinking beer in a pub. As shocking as that fact is, then I have to confess to being even more surprised to see you dressed as you are, and the long hair, and so on, and so forth," the man said as he waved his hands in the air toward me as if to encompass my entire appearance and the world and aura around me.

Yes, in-deedy, here we go.

This was gonna be fun!

I cast a quick glimpse at Jennifer, who was walking back to our end of the bar while carrying some dirty glasses and empty plates. The gorgeous bartender had heard just enough of the man's words and seen the man's hands waving in my direction to follow the general gist of this conversation. Jennifer rolled her eyes a little while, nodding in the direction of the wash sink. I could tell by the body motions and nods that Jennifer was going to wash the glassware and dishes and give me some space to cool the man's jets just a bit. Nothing like being on your own. But Jennifer knew that I could and would hold my own with this man. I too have been down this road before and I figured that I might just as well launch his ass to the moon without a rocket ship right away. I leaned forward, pulled my wallet out of my back pocket, and removed one of my business cards. No sense in prolonging the truth on this one.

"Here is my business card. Despite my actual position, I do much prefer the title of Pastor Paul."

The man did not follow the remark; there was no reason for him to do so until he saw my actual title. I leaned over and the man placed his glass on the bar top, leaned over and took the business card from my hand. When he leaned back onto the stool and I did the same to mine, I waited for his reaction when he spotted the bishop title printed on my card. His brow furrowed, his mouth screwed shut while he studied the card, and I could tell that he was struggling with the bishop title. As he struggled, I tried very hard to figure out what his angle was going to be. It was obvious that he had an issue with my appearance, as well as the fact that I was enjoying a beer or two. It was then that I noticed, or rather surmised by the appearance of the glass, that his drink was either water or a soda.

Supposition abounds!

In self-defense, I delved into the memory banks and, as I often did in these types of situations, tapped the vast knowledge of my own father's keen and remarkable mind. My old man was the King of New Jersey Street Sense and often his ability to label and diagnose a situation was not only precise but incredibly poignant too. It was as if the old man channeled me, because loud and clear in my head, the name that he often used for overzealous religious persons, popped into my mind.

"Bible Thumper," the old man said to me.

'Thanks, Dad. Let's see if we are correct or not.'

I also recalled his famous motto and warning, "Never discuss money, religion, or politics. Especially in a gin joint."

Perfect advice, except for the fact that my current profession and vows made skipping discussing religion nearly impossible. I really tried to fly under the radar with my attire and hiding out here and to try to enjoy a quiet afternoon, but it looked as if this conversation just thwarted my plans.

"This makes it all the worse. A bishop in the Lutheran Church? Really? And you are carrying on as you do? My goodness, this is a tragedy and just another reason that I chose to forego the mainstream denominations and be ordained in a nondenominational church that remains faithful to the Bible." In apparent disgust, he shook his head, and while he took what appeared to be the last bite of his sandwich, the man mumbled, "Pastor Douglas Wright. Senior Pastor of the Light of the World Bible Church." He offered no business card, and I watched and laughed just a little when he casually tossed my card aside as if it was poison.

I leaned back and whispered, "You nailed it, Dad."

Yes, there go my plans for a quiet afternoon!

To add to my shock and horror factor and exemplify my status as a sinner, I caught Jennifer's eyes and smiled while asking, "Please a refill."

Jennifer, now knowing my method of operation, smiled and tossed her dishrag aside while grabbing a fresh mug out of the chiller.

"Of course, precious," Jennifer announced as she drew another Big Boulder from the tap. Most of the bar now emptied of patrons, and it would most likely remain empty until the dinner crowd rolled in. While I did not really want to engage the pastor in a Bible debate, deep down as a former professional athlete, there remained inside of me a competitive edge. I shrugged off the initial reactions and waited for the attack to arrive.

And so, it goes.

"Another beer, huh? I suppose this is how a bishop flaunts his life away, by staring into the bottom of another empty beer mug and cavorting with pretty bartenders."

This pastor was blasting away at me now. No holds barred in his opinions.

I smiled as Jennifer delivered the beer and leaned in close to me. Oh, so well, she knew the look in my eyes and since there remained no other guests, Jennifer decided to sit in for a ringside seat. To this old hockey goaltender, it was a game on now!

"I find it interesting that you are so judgmental. Yet, you sit here at the bar in a pub too."

Upon hearing my words, his mouth turned down into a

moue and he waved his hand across the dining area of the pub's floor.

Pastor Wright now assumed a defensive posture while saying, "I was running late, I was very hungry, and when I arrived—only this seat at the bar was available. The tables were all full."

I nodded at his rather defensive explanation and since I had him wobbling a bit, I decided to dig in a little more.

"Let me point out that Jesus turned the water into wine to keep the party going and I choose to follow the Gospel rather than mire in the writings of Saint Paul and his highly selective opinions. Strong drink is a brawler. Martin Luther's wife was a well-known expert brewer in Germany. Martin Luther often accepted payment for his work in kegs of beer, but wrote home to Mrs. Luther how the quality never compared to his wife's brews."

Pastor Wright frowned, and he pointed at his glass while proudly proclaiming, "This is soda."

It seemed as if he was going to choose to ignore the fact that Jesus drank wine and partied in celebration of this weird thing, we all call life.

Then, with a huff and more than a bit of puff, he explained, "I choose to follow the teachings of Paul above other writings. Paul was inspired by the Holy Spirit and he expounded on the Gospel."

Now, I dug in, "Pauline Christianity is dangerous and, in many ways, contrary to the Gospel of Jesus. Paul is not Jesus, our Lord and Savior. Paul is a preacher. As we are. What it seems is that, as a Bible Fundamentalist, all that you do, is to pick and choose Saint Paul's teachings and other verses and you use them where they fit into your beliefs and self-promotions of your own specific agendas. Paul was writing in a specific time and place, to his friends and ministers struggling to establish the church from grass roots. Please take time to be careful when you use his work to overrule the Gospel or the Old Testament. I often stop at

Acts. No reason to go much farther. Just my opinion."

"The Old Testament was replaced by the New Covenant. Man, mires in Original Sin. The New Covenant is our savior. Even babies in the womb are doomed before birth. They inherited sin from Adam and are doomed without the New Covenant. The Catholic Church is wrong because even the Virgin Mary was a sinner because she called Jesus, her Savior."

Oh, boy, the Original Sin theory and this one made my skin crawl. Jennifer rolled her eyes, and she picked up her bar rag and began to wipe down the bar counter.

I shook my head and asked a question that I already knew the answer to.

"Where and how where you ordained, Pastor Wright?"

"I am self-ordained and the leader of a vibrant, Bible believing congregation that supports my ministry and promotes the Gospel."

I cut him off, "Who's Gospel, yours or Christ's?"

Then the label that my old boss, the late, great Bishop Werner Beck Von Houten placed upon these types of pastors came into my mind, "Do it yourselfers." While I understood Bishop Von Houten's meaning and respected his opinions, I have met many amazing and wonderful self-ordained pastors. Pastors that I had great respect for and deep admiration for their work and mission. I did not feel as though paperwork hanging on a wall made you a qualified person to promote the work of God. It was the spirit within your heart that counts. Yet, I could tell by this man's attitude, by his obvious disdain for me and my actions and all that I stood for, that he was a bit too close-minded and exceedingly self-righteous. Not to mention overly judgmental of me, without knowing anything about me other than my appearance, my love of beer and my friendship with a gorgeous woman.

Let's see now if we could make an attitude adjustment or two.

I held back a laugh as Pastor Wright pondered my question; I took a long sip of beer and then spoke before the answer arrived, "Jesus came to fulfill and to support the Old Testament, not to abolish it. He was Jewish and never pretended to be anything other than Jewish. Your Gospel, beg my pardon, and in due respect, is flawed. Inheriting Adam's sin is contrary to everything that The Bible teaches about a loving, caring God and voids the teachings of every prophet. I do mean every Prophet from Moses, to Daniel, to Abraham, to Mohammed, to Jesus. How does a loving God condemn an unborn and innocent baby? God stopped Abraham before he sacrificed his beloved son, and Jesus did not find sin with the woman about to receive a stoning. In my honest opinion, it is a ridiculous theory. The Bible does not directly teach it, instead, it is a theory patched together by early interpreters of scripture. I cannot find anywhere in scripture where Jesus directly supported it, Judaism and other religions do not support it and I do not either. It is contrary to the message of love. Frankly and gruffly, the thought of Original Sin, is man-made bullshit."

Pastor Wright seemed ruffled by my passionate response and my harsh words and he too dug in with a fact, "Martin Luther promoted Original Sin as a correct theory."

"Right you are, Luther felt strongly about the concept. As did Calvin, and I disagree with them both on this subject. In my honest opinion, it is a false interpretation of Saint Paul's writings. I do not lock step with all the teachings of Lutheranism and I do not agree with all the work of Martin Luther. For example, some of his writings and opinions of the Jewish people in Germany fueled way too horrific a fire. Those writings are wretched, and I am all too proud to say that I disagree with them and stand firmly against them. Just as with Saint Paul's writings, Luther was writing at a certain time and place. We must be careful in our studies and use all of scripture for a cross check of the verification of our beliefs, not just pick out individual parts and pieces."

The pastor had no response and instead, he waved rather impolitely to Jennifer to refill his soda. Jennifer walked silently over to where he sat. She picked up his glass and then walked away to refill it, while the pastor shook his head and carefully watched Jennifer as she walked away. It was easy to read his mind, and I added my opinion in there to fuel his fire a little. There was little doubt that I was enjoying this.

"As far as my appearance is concerned, and my so-called cavorting with the lovely bartender who by the way, is not pretty, but she is gorgeous, I am my own man, made in the image that God desires and I do not judge, so you should not judge either. No reason to cast stones first, eh? In his day, Jesus was unconventional, and no one was more unconventional than John the Baptist was. I am what I am. Nothing special, a man who falls short every day, but I am my own man. My wife always told me to stay as I wanted to be and I do. I am now a widower. My wife has been gone for many years now. I have lost track out of fear of the pain of the memory. Jennifer is one of my closest friends. We love each other in a God glorifying manner, just as Jesus loved Mary Magdalene and was not ashamed to say it and display his love too. I truly believe that Mary Magdalene was the thirteenth disciple, and in many ways, Mary might have been the most important one. Jesus revealed his raised human body to her first for a very good reason."

After speaking, I picked up the beer mug and took a long sip while I felt his eyes carefully studying me. I winked at Jennifer as I placed the mug onto the bar top and she smiled as I watched her body relax and her tension ease. Before continuing to speak, I fiddled with the handle of the beer mug and then turned and faced Pastor Wright and spoke openly and honestly. Despite the pain of this week, I felt as if I needed to do so and thought that this might help cleanse me of this recent pain.

"Jennifer has supported me through some very difficult times, and I will forever be grateful to her for her love, kindness, and amazing friendship. Love glorifies God and love neutralizes hate. It is the primary message of the Gospel and The Bible and of most faiths and religions. Simple love without all kinds of rules and man-made regulations and interpretations hanging upon our hearts. The love of God, love of our fellow humankind, love of Jesus and all the Major Prophets and love for this glorious world. God existed before humankind created organized religion. Love conquers all of that madness. It lays bare our soul, extends the joy of our daily existence, and is God's greatest gift to us."

Jennifer smiled at me and tears clearly appeared in her eyes as she walked back over to Pastor Wright and delivered the refilled soda.

"This is on the house, Pastor Wright. I will proudly tell you that I love Pastor Paul, with all my heart and soul. Some people see a shapely bartender, tilting mugs, slinging and mixing drinks, accepting sly and disgusting comments from unruly drunk men trying to get lucky with what they perceive to be an available woman and trying to pinch my ass when I walk by them. Their drunken lust reduces me to simply being eye candy for idiots. Pastor Paul sees my heart and my soul and not the woman that I want people to see, but the woman that I want to be seen as."

Pastor Wright nodded.

He still did not thank Jennifer, but he took his glass of soda and lifted it to his lips to take a long drink. It seemed as if he was pondering all of what transpired. I watched his eyes as he carefully followed Jennifer's glorious body while she glided across the floor and over to where I sat. I am sure his eyes were wide open as Jennifer once more came over by me, leaned in and gently grasped my hands while she kissed me once again, gently and carefully. For the first time, I think Pastor Wright's heart softened for a bit and he finally spoke as I lifted the beer mug to my lips and took a long sip.

Pastor Wright spoke, this time in a softer voice and a gentler manner, "You are quite a powerful speaker, Pastor Paul. Quite interesting too. You speak with some very emotional and powerful words and with great insight into human souls. You are intelligent, gifted, honest and forthright and I take note that you are liberal in some of your thoughts but highly conservative in others. You seem to be ecumenical and envelope the teachings of all religions. I suppose that holds some merit even if they are all flawed and Christianity is the only true ticket to Heaven. Regardless, I respect your opinions and admire your speaking abilities."

I nodded as his eyes darted around the barroom as he took note of his surroundings and gathered his thoughts. Rather than thank him for his praise, I held my tongue, because it was obvious that the pastor had some more to say.

He did, and again Pastor Wright's voice was soft and low, "I am sorry to hear of your wife's passing. Very, very sorry. If it is not too painful, might I ask, was it an illness? Could not strong and powerful prayer save her situation or the laying of hands cure her ills?"

I answered his questions without a second of hesitation.

"It was a tragic and horrific car crash. My wife died instantly."

Pastor Wright almost dropped his glass, and he seemed to be stunned.

After struggling with what seemed to be some shock mixed in with some regrets for his attacks on me, Pastor Wright said, "Oh my, and yet, your faith remains powerful and strong and you remain in your bishop's position and do God's work?"

"I do. It was not easy. I fought with God for quite a long time, until I gained acceptance. Honestly, our loss here on Earth simply became Heaven's gain. God's plan is not always, what we want, or desire or agree with, yet, I follow it, often blindly, but I follow. Even Jesus asked at the base of the cross if there might be another way and then Jesus understood and he accepted God's plan."

I paused and held back some emotions while fiddling again with the handle of the beer mug.

"Every day, I write to my wife. I write random notes with random thoughts and I keep them all in a journal. I call them my chronicles. Sometimes, I open the book and reread them, but honestly, most times, I write them, place them in the book and never revisit them again."

With a quick flip of my wrist, I grabbed the paper with my daily notes on it, held it up for Pastor Wright to see, and then placed it back down on the bar top. Pastor Wright glanced at the note, and I could see his eyes begin to glisten as he studied my words.

"Since my beloved wife left this world, I have become very introverted. I keep a very small circle of friends. Obviously . . . Jennifer is one of them. Our children comfort me, my sister, and other remaining family, along with a few other close friends. They are the joy in my life that keeps me upright. God's Grace and love, power me to plow onward and ever upward. Despite the glorious love that surrounds me, for the most part, other than work, I enjoy being alone with my thoughts. The quiet times are very enjoyable. My writing helps me deal with the pain and allows me to think and believe that my beloved wife is still close to me, guiding me, holding my soul within her loving heart and bringing my woes and prayers to all the saints in Heaven that reside with her. That is what I was doodling here on this pad while I ate my supper and enjoyed a few beers. They are notes now, but when I am finished, it will be a letter to my wife."

Pastor Wright nodded, and for the first time, he smiled. Now, with the lights of the bar and the afternoon sun chasing into the windows, it was obvious that tears filled his eyes. He took a bar napkin and dabbed at his eyes.

I heard him mumble, "Heaven's gain. That is an extraordinary thought."

He stood up, walked over and it was then that I saw he was very short and indeed, he was quite overweight. I thought how the soda was not helping his weight issues, but, Pastor Paul, please cast no stones here.

His lively religious zeal and his animation and forcefulness seemed to be missing now, and he seemed shaken by our conversation and the entire experience. I jumped off the bar stool and Pastor Wright was immediately surprised by my height and size. I towered over the little man.

"My goodness, I had no idea that you were so tall, muscular and, well . . .imposing."

"My pleasure to meet you, Pastor Wright. Please, my yoke is easy and I assure you that despite my situation, my burden is now very light. The Grace of God keeps me upright. I must say that I greatly enjoyed the Biblical debate and wish you all the best of luck with your mission and with your church. Grace and peace to you. May the love of God guide the ways of your heart and the footsteps of your life."

Pastor Wright held my hand for quite a long time and he looked in my eyes for the same amount of time, before he finally said, "I will dip into a touch of Lutheranism here. And, also with you, Pastor Paul. Please forgive me for my hasty and incorrect prejudgment of you. You have taught me a great deal in a very short amount of time. You have taught me about blind faith. You have taught me what faith really means when faith exists solely within your heart. You have taught me about the love of God. Reinforced the Gospel lesson of casting stones. You are a man of God. It has been my pleasure. Truly, it has been."

Pastor Wright let go of my hand, turned, and spun away from me. I have to say that he seemed as if he was in a bit of a daze of some sort. He stopped by his stool, reached in his wallet and dropped a wad of cash on the bar top, waved and smiled at Jennifer and he grabbed my business card and tucked it in his suit jacket pocket.

With a mumbled, "Thank you" to Jennifer, and a quick glance my way, he turned and briskly walked out of the front door of, "The Elusive Lion Public House."

Jennifer walked over, picked up the money and thumbed through it as she checked the amount versus the tab.

"Well, dear, Jennifer?" I asked. My curiosity as to the amount was obvious.

"Wow, he left me an amazing tip," Jennifer said with a huge element of surprise in her voice. I felt a little shiver ripple inside of my soul at the sight of her smile and her beauty.

Perhaps, as far as my relationship with Jennifer goes, God just led me in a different direction.

"Rightly so. You are the best of the best. You earned it today, for sure. Did you mention before that you get off at six? I did have plans, but I will call Heather Sarah and tell her that I have made other plans for tonight. She will understand when I give her the details and I dare say that she will be quite happy to hear of them, too. How about dinner and a movie and afterwards, then whatever happens, kinda happens, eh? I am not sure that I am ready for any romance in my life, but I always have room for an amazing friend such as you are."

Jennifer smiled. She fussed with her hair, and then playfully, tugged at her neckline to reveal a bit of her ample cleavage to me and said, "Yes, off at six. Give me time to go home, clean up and make myself pretty."

"Ha! You could never be anything else but gorgeous,

inside and outside. However, if you need it, let's make it seven or so. I will pick you up. Geez, in the end, time will mean very little to any of us. Right?"

"Right. Paul, you melt my heart with your immaculate looks and your incredible honor. Time spent with you, my dear Paul, is as if I drink some type of magic potion that cures all the ills of my soul. You are magical in so many ways. It is as if you broadcast some glorious music on a wavelength of love. Dinner and a movie, and whatever happens, geez, my goodness, you turn me inside and out too. What a beautiful man you are. Honestly, I thought that you would never suggest such an evening to me!"

About six months or so thereafter, the encounter, the discussion, and experience with Pastor Douglas Wright, I was sitting in my office going through the daily mail that Martha had placed in my "in box." After carefully checking and sorting it, I picked up an envelope stamped with the return address of, "Light of the World Bible Church."

At first, the return address meant very little to me and then the ghosts shook it loose, and in an instant, I rewound the memory in my mind. I then recalled the glorious evening that Jennifer and I spent together. Believe me when I say that it was very easy for me to recall all of the details of that evening. My goodness, Jennifer is gorgeous in so many ways and what we shared that evening was beyond glorious too.

Of interest to me was the fact that the envelope had used the title of "Pastor Paul John Henson" in the address. No bishop title and I remained sure that I had mentioned to Pastor Wright that I did not enjoy the use of the bishop title and preferred to use the title of Pastor Paul. While I reached for my letter opener, I thought how Pastor Wright was a perceptive and respectful chap to have caught and to have honored that wish.

A tear or two of the paper envelope revealed a carefully typed letter.

Pastor Paul,

I have to take the time to write to you and thank you for the discussion that we had that afternoon in the pub in downtown Newark. I was in Newark to sign off on some legal papers for a real estate deal for my church and my schedule and hunger caused me to wander around to find a place to eat. The pub caught my eye, and the rest is history. Ordinarily, my prior beliefs and stiff mannerisms would steer me clear of anything to do with a pub. Now, I do realize that God led me to meet Jennifer and Pastor Paul John Henson. I truly hope that Jennifer and you accept my sincere apology for my poor behavior and that you accept my apology for my hasty judgment of you, based solely upon your outward appearance, the fact that you were drinking beer and sharing time with the lovely Jennifer. I was wrong in so many ways and your passion, your words, your insight, and your quiet power caused me to stop, pause, and reexamine my life, and, honestly, my preaching. It was an awakening for me.

A glorious awakening.

The awakening.

I have you to thank for it. After we met, and I had some time to digest the many points that you spoke to me, the love you displayed to me, for your wife, combined with Jennifer's testimony, and then I knew that I was too close-minded and needed to change much of what I was doing and teaching too. I researched you and read many of your books and writings. They are all amazing and insightful too. My self-examination was deep and powerful and honestly performed with your assistance and God's unlimited Grace. I feel as if I am now back on track, and much more open-minded. The Gospel of Jesus is the true Gospel and I understand what it was that you taught to me.

Furthermore, upon extensive research and prayer, I feel as if a little baby does not inherit sin.

Let me quote, and please forgive me, if I do not detail it all correctly, "Love glorifies God and love neutralizes hate. It is the primary message of the Gospel and The Bible and of most faiths and religions. Simple love without all kinds of rules and man-made regulations and interpretations hanging upon our hearts. The love of God, love of our fellow humankind, love of Jesus and all the Major Prophets and love for this glorious world. God existed before humankind created organized religion. Love conquers all of that madness. It lays bare our soul, extends the joy of our daily existence, and is God's greatest gift to us."

In addition, any loss of our loved ones here on Earth simply becomes, "Heaven's gain."

Thank you, Pastor Paul, and even if we never meet again until we meet in Heaven, then thank you for you.

In the service of The Lord,

Mr. Douglas Wright.

I closed the letter and pondered it a bit.

The awakening. Very nice.

Strange, but he did not use the title of a pastor when he signed the letter. Instead, he was Mister Douglas Wright. Very interesting. No longer a "do it yourselfer?"

I am not sure, but regardless, he was, and is, a man of God. Titles mean nothing to me and I am sure that God has no title cards on file either. I hope that Mr. Wright was back on course and if I managed to contribute in some manner, then all the best for this world and for his congregation. Believers are believers and the love of God has no boundary.

While placing the letter back into the envelope and into my "tickler" file, my mind wandered and returned to that day and that night. I tried hard to prevent my thoughts from wandering too much, but I couldn't help but to recall how wonderful a day it was and all that we shared. Not only with Mr. Douglas Wright, but for Jennifer and me too.

I looked at my watch and noted the time. I might be able to catch Jennifer before her shift ended. I will call her in a minute and see what her plans are for after her shift ends.

All in good time. First, I just needed to finish this note that I started on my daily letter to Binky.

When I see Jennifer and discuss the letter, and all of my thoughts associated with that remarkable day, and I tell her how I feel about the details of the evening that was even more remarkable, my hope is that Jennifer will share in my thoughts and enthusiasm.

In fact, I know that she will.

You see, I know, Jennifer knows, and in my heart, I hope and I pray that the world knows that love conquers all of that madness. It lays bare our soul, extends the joy of our daily existence, and is God's greatest gift to us.

THE END

Letter Four

Beloved Wife,

Sometimes, with this modern technology, I want to hit the "select all" and then erase everything that I wrote. I do mean, dear Binky, everything. I mean to go back to the first word that I ever typed and erase all of it.

Nothing makes the cut.

Nothing.

I think that the material is very weak and often poorly composed. Then, I re-examine all of the words and I feel the words and the power of them. I mean, I put my fingers on the keyboard of this old laptop and I feel the raw emotion of the words. The fact that I wrote these words with all of my heart and soul and the fact that our love, our life, my love for God, and for Rose and for Harry, and for all of our children, and all of our friends and our loved ones, transposes into my fingers. It is then that I know to erase all of these words would be a tragic error. These are more than simply words that I wrote here in these volumes of books. No, no, no, it is much more than just words.

I have left my heart and my soul on these pages.

Maybe, my skills as an author do not allow me to write with the most glorious of words, or perhaps, I am not able to mold them together and compose them in the grandest style of writing. I admit that fact, but my writing is heartfelt, and if I were to erase these words, then I would have erased parts of our lives and our love. That would be a grave error, because above all, I want the world to know of our lives together and of our love.

Words are the tools of my trade now and they are all that I have to give and, in some ways, all that I have left of you and of me.

I write onward, dear Binky, and always and forever, I will never erase all that we shared and all that we were and are.

Always and forever, our love lives in these words.

You have my word and my honor that in our lives there are no such things as "erase" buttons.

Time to go now, more words to write.

More ghosts to chase away.

Love Always,

#27

Ashes

Pastor Wilhelm Bruckermann opened the door to the bishop's office, and I looked up from my work to see him look at me, force a weak smile, wave, and then quickly walk over to my assistant, Ms. Martha Wiggin's desk. I looked at the clock on the wall of my office and checked the time. Ten minutes to one in the afternoon. The prediction in my mind that dear Martha would let him know that it was ten minutes to the hour, and that she would remind Pastor Bruckermann that his appointment was for one o'clock, took about four microseconds to come to fruition.

In fact, maybe three microseconds.

"You are early, Pastor Bruckermann. Please, have a seat and I will let Pastor Paul know that you are here and I will also put you down for a new watch for Christmas."

Upon overhearing her comments, I smiled and chuckled at my faithful assistant's aggressiveness and somewhat overly protective approach to my schedule, my workday, and me. Martha Wiggins felt that I worked too hard and too many hours, and she always defended me as the bulldog that she was.

Pastor Bruckermann stumbled and started his response a number of times while Martha waved her hand dismissively at the guest chair in the main office and told the befuddled pastor, "Have a seat and relax on your ass for a few minutes. Pastor Paul is a busy man. If you would like a cup of coffee, I can get it, but only after I answer this email to this clueless pastor who never can submit a budget correctly."

"Ah, yes, okay, thank you, Ms. Wiggins, and I do not need a cup of coffee. Say, might I ask—are my budgets correct?"

Martha leaned in over her desk and in her fabulously forthright and honest manner asked, "Have you ever received a scathing email from me, laced with profanity and berating words in response to one of your budget submittals?"

"No, I do not ever recall receiving such an email."

Martha sat back and smiled and with a direct and forceful voice Martha said, "Then, we are good."

I loved me some Martha Wiggins.

I heard Martha's fingernails furiously tapping away on her keyboard, and shortly thereafter, I saw the messenger box on my computer screen light up with a text message.

With a tilt, a smile and a lean, I leaned in and read it, "The pastor with a long last name is here for your one o'clock. EARLY!!!!"

After fiddling around a few minutes in order to kill some time on the clock, I thought, okay, now, it is time to save the good pastor from Martha. I did not want to jump the gun early and face the wrath of Martha, but I also needed to save a fellow man of the cloth. It was now four minutes to the hour, and even dear Martha allowed for some wiggle room. I rose from my chair and walked out to greet Pastor Bruckermann.

With my hand extended, I first thanked Martha for her amazing efficiency, which resulted in a raise of her eyebrows and a mumbled, "Harrumph."

Then, as Pastor Bruckermann rose from his chair, I shook his hand and warmly greeted Pastor Wilhelm Bruckermann, "Nice to see you, Wilhelm. It has been a bit of time since I have seen you. My apologies, my schedule never eases."

He was young, my best guess would be in his mid-thirties or thereabouts. I suppose that I could check his human resource file, but what did it matter? Age was simply a measuring stick. He was immaculately dressed in a black suit with a traditional white clerical collar around his neck. He was a young Lutheran pastor, slightly nervous in his actions, and still inexperienced in his career. If I recalled correctly, he entered the ministry after a short career as a civil engineer. He was a little on the short side in height, but lean and clean-shaven, with a full head of dirty blonde hair that he wore on the longish side. His green eyes darted first to my hand and then he turned his attention to thanking Martha.

"Thank you, Ms. Wiggins. No need for a watch. Mine works fine."

"Okay. So, noted. Use it then. And, you are welcome," Martha said while she pecked away on the keyboard.

I smiled at Martha's comments, and the young pastor forced a smile.

As we shook hands and turned toward my office, Pastor Bruckermann said, "Nice to see you too, Pastor Paul. No trouble. I understand the demands for your time. I appreciate you fitting me in here today."

No doubt, he was quite nervous and very upset about something, and even though Martha meant no harm and was simply being "Martha," I am sure that she did not help with Pastor Bruckermann's general disposition.

A careful study of his face told me that this was not going to be a general visit. Something tragic and severe weighed heavily on the young pastor's mind. Wilhelm looked very young, but somehow, since the last time we visited, he seemed to have aged considerably. His furrowed brow, the deep lines on his face, his slow gait. . ..

This was a concerned and troubled man. As we entered my office, and I offered him my guest chair, I prayed a quick and silent prayer that I might help him with whatever it was that brought him to my office this afternoon.

Pastor Wilhelm Bruckermann served a mid-sized church with a rather active congregation located in Rockland County, New York. I had visited his church a number of times. The congregation was vibrant, a little younger in age than many other Lutheran congregations in the district and from all indications, Pastor Wilhelm was doing a fine job. The church was located just over the New Jersey border and while it was not a long drive from his parish to my office here in Newark, New Jersey, I am sure that due to the usual traffic madness of the area that it was not an entirely pleasant ride either. If I recalled correctly, Pastor Bruckermann had rural Pennsylvania roots and the metro area roads can be quite intimidating.

In the interest of breaking the tension, I offered him some refreshment and some small talk.

"I know that you told Martha that you did not want any coffee, but do you want tea, or perhaps, some water? By the way, did you find some parking close by?"

He waved in the air to indicate, "No," to any refreshments, and then he added, "I parked in the parking garage a few blocks away. It was a short walk, and I needed the fresh air. I parked where Martha told me to park. She is very, how do I put this . . . efficient."

"She means no harm. Martha guards me like a bulldog, but she is full of God's love and is supremely committed to our mission. I would be lost without her help and her endless dedication. We have been together forever and perhaps, just a little longer than forever."

Another nod of the head and a forced smile.

Okay, got it. Time to get right to it. The purpose of this visit. I settled into my chair, turned off my computer to minimize any distraction, and then turned my full attention to the young man seated before me. God spoke to my heart to focus.

"What brings you here today, Pastor Bruckermann?

How can I help?"

His eyes nervously darted around.

He paused and asked, "Can we close the door to your office?"

I stood my ground on this one. After all, I was a long-haired hippie pastor, but I was his boss.

"No, please, I am fine and you should be, too. I have no secrets with Martha. I assure you that Martha holds everything within our mission. As I just said, Martha is full of God's love."

A nod in agreement. A deep breath. Pain on full display and then a long exhale.

"I need to leave the ministry." I turned my mouth up and slowly nodded, not sure of the next words to speak, but Pastor Bruckermann spoke first, "I have failed God and I have failed my wife and family because of my inadequacies at my calling."

After dropping the bomb as a reason for his visit, I picked up a pencil off my desk, leaned back in my chair, and slowly nodded my head. This certainly was not going to be a Mr. Bluebird happily chirping on my shoulder type of day. Silence ensued; Pastor Wilhelm coughed a nervous cough and fidgeted in his chair, while not making direct eye contact with me, but keeping me in his sights.

"I see. Okay, well, this news certainly comes as a huge surprise. What has led you to such a weighty and life-changing decision?"

"This is the hardest thing that I have ever had to say to anyone and I know that you are the bishop, my managerial boss, so to speak and that . . . you are also a fellow pastor . . . and a man, but it is still hard to speak about and to even think of. I am going crazy with emotional pain." As soon as the words left his lips, tears formed in the corners of his eyes, and he grabbed his hair and wrung his hands through it while he jumped from the chair. He began to pace rather nervously in front of my desk and quickly, his tears turned into rounds of a full-fledged sobbing.

"Easy, now, Pastor Wilhelm. Easy now, God will give you comfort and we will stand with you," I said while I jumped up and walked over to him. While putting my arm around his shoulders, I gently led him over to another set of chairs set on opposite sides of a small table that I set up in my office. It was a place where I often sat with persons in order to eliminate the impersonal feeling of the desk setting. On the table, I kept a Bible, a box of tissues and a small table lamp. The illumination from the lamp was low, and the shade glowed with a soothing light. One of the chairs was very old, but it was a special chair given to me as a gift by a very special friend many years earlier. It had an aura of comfort to it, a remarkable warmth, and when you sat in the chair, the arms held you in an envelopment of protection and provided you love mixed with comfort. I knew that I had to pull out all my secret weapons from Pastor Paul's arsenal for this discussion.

I had one more secret weapon in the stash.

"Come on now, over here. Let's sit here. It is more comfortable. Please, take this chair. It is a very special chair."

He nodded, but his sobs made his body violently shake and his hands trembled. As soon as he sat in the chair, he reached for the box of tissues and began to clean up.

"I will be right back."

I walked over to the open doorway of my office and turned to Martha. Because, as she often reminds me, she is the world's greatest assistant, and we had been together forever, Martha already was obtaining what I needed from the arsenal. Martha actually kept this weapon hidden from me for quite a long time until strategically revealing it for deployment one day during an unusual meeting here in the office. Martha opened the drawer of her file cabinet, pulled out the bottle of Scotch whiskey and then grabbed two shot glasses from inside the cupboard in the refreshment area of our offices. She turned and smiled when I held up three fingers and waved her over. Martha grabbed a third glass. We walked in the office. Pastor Wilhelm looked up, and while his body no longer shook and his sobbing had eased, he still looked like a man in shock. I could not even imagine what had brought this young man to this point in his life, but unless he pulled it together, it was going to be difficult to assist him in his plight. We set the shot glasses on the table and Martha handed me the bottle. Pastor Bruckermann studied our actions, but he did not say a single word.

I poured three shots, handed the harried pastor a shot, and said, "Here. This will steady you out some. Please."

He took the glass, nodded in agreement, tilted it over, and sent it on its happy way. I handed Martha a glass, and she did the same, as did I. Martha reached to retrieve the bottle and empty shot glasses and I gently placed my hand over her hand.

"Please, leave it, dear Martha."

Then, as the whiskey warmed my soul, I felt very strongly that I needed Martha here with us for this discussion. Pastor Bruckermann had experienced her tough and difficult side, but now, I felt as if I needed her extraordinary insight into life and her special touch of love.

"Please, Martha, roll a chair over here. I need you, and Pastor Wilhelm needs you too. God just spoke to my heart."

Once more, Pastor Wilhelm only studied me, but he did not say a word. Martha seemed to be a bit surprised at my request, but since the pastor did not object, she nodded, grabbed one of the guest chairs and rolled it over to where we sat.

"Feeling a bit better?" I asked.

Now he tried to smile and mumbled, "Yes, I am. So sorry for the loss of composure, but I am gaining strength now." He picked up the empty shot glass and held it in the air and now he successfully smiled and managed to say, "Thank you both."

We sat in silence for a few seconds, until he cleared his throat and now, under some semblance of composure, he spilled the story.

With a wipe of his eyes, he said, "Well, guess I need to get right to it. I have become obsessed with my pastoral mission. Honestly, I have buried myself in the work and calling, devoting all my waking hours to the church and leaving little time for my wife and daughter. When I return home, it seems as if I am so emotionally and physically exhausted that I cannot even interact with them. I eat and collapse in bed just to get up and do it over again the next day."

I nodded and said, "Do you take Fridays off?"

Friday was the traditional day for pastors to take off to allow some sort of "weekend" before the Sunday crush.

Pastor Wilhelm shook his head and said, "No. I usually work on Saturdays too."

Martha's eyes looked over at me, and she leaned into her chair. Martha was with me for many years when I served as Senior Pastor at Reunion Lutheran Church. In fact, I was the only pastor, senior or otherwise, and I trapped myself in the same pattern of work that the young pastor just testified to us. Martha warned me many times, and when I hit my own doldrums and skids, I woke up soon enough to crawl out of it and change my lifestyle and work patterns. I knew from the look on her face that Martha knew that I was qualified to relate to his situation.

With a cavalier attitude, I launched into some round of blabber and bullshit as if I had walked in Pastor Wilhelm's shoes, "I understand. When I was the pastor at Reunion Lutheran Church, I fell into the same trap and I made my wife and family suffer as a result of my intense. . .."

He abruptly cut me off and almost shouted as he leaned in and confessed, "Suffer! You made your family suffer!

Really? So much that your beautiful, young wife felt so abandoned that she went and had an extra-marital affair with one of our most active parishioners and now is pregnant with his child?"

Martha gasped, and I fell back into the chair. If Mr. Bluebird was on my shoulder, he keeled over too. After recovering, Martha jumped up, grabbed the bottle, and immediately poured us three more shots. I knew that I had made the correct choice by asking Martha to stay. After another round, it was easy to see that between the whiskey and the outpouring of the truth from deep within his soul, Pastor Wilhelm felt some sort of relief. I cannot even imagine the turmoil in his soul, and I prayed silently for guidance with this situation. This one was a whopper of a mess. I wiped my mouth after downing the shot of whiskey and mouthed a thank you to dear Martha, whose face, despite the shot of liquid warmth working away at her insides, was ashen.

"Well, I see . . . okay, well, let's see what we can do here in order to sort it all out now, Pastor Wilhelm," I stammered and sputtered while searching for the correct words and some kind of direction.

The liquid courage propelled the good pastor as he took the lead.

"It is all my fault. I led her into another man's arms. I failed as a father, a husband, and a man of God. Donald is a stalwart in the church, he serves on many committees and he is young, dynamic, and strikingly handsome. I am frumpy, not overly handsome or appealing, slightly boring and lost in my work. My wife is younger than I am and she is beautiful, vibrant and outgoing. I am introverted and I should have known that I could never keep her. When my wife and Donny took the lead on a mission committee and spent quite a bit of time together, or I should clarify and say that they spent quite a bit of quality time together, while I ignored her, then she was smitten. One late evening of committee work led to another, and while I was busy with making myself a hero to Saint Mark's Lutheran Church, she found passion and comfort in his arms. I am a fool, and now, I want to leave this mess behind."

"You are not a fool. Their sins are not the result of you being a fool. I can assure you of that. You might have been driven, commanding and overly committed in your mission, but you are not a fool," I said as I paused and studied Pastor Wilhelm's face and it was easy to tell that he was not buying what it was that I was selling. The next question was one that I had to ask, but I knew that I would regret hearing the answer, as I had a deep feeling that I already knew the answer beforehand.

"Is this Donny chap married, too?"

Without a second of hesitation, Pastor Wilhelm answered, "Yes, he is. Luckily, unlike us, they have no children. His is a classic case of he loves his wife but is not in love with her. At least that is what he told Valerie . . . my wife's name is Valerie. He is in love only with Valerie and my wife says that she loves him too." For a brief second, I thought that we were going to lose him again to tears and despair, while his eyes rolled in his head and his mouth quivered, but he recovered enough to proclaim, "All I have left now are ashes. My life is nothing but ashes."

I shook my head and heard Martha deeply exhale. On the messy meter, this sucker was pegging the needle all the way to the "horrible" side. Despite the persona, clergy are not immune to the madness and evils of life. In this case, Pastor Wilhelm was twisting and turning within the deepest grip of madness that life could throw at him. Yet, when I looked into his eyes, I did not see a beaten man. Instead, I saw a man who now had learned from his mistakes, and a man who now was ready to rise from the ashes and regroup.

It was time to ask the wretched question, "I have to ask, but as a man and as a pastor my question is, are you sure that Donny is the father of the child? Can this be without a doubt?"

Pastor Wilhelm answered quickly and without any elements of the slightest doubt in his voice, "It is Donny's child. Valerie and I were not intimate for a very long time. I was an idiot who was always too tired and too wound up to meet the basic sexual needs of a young, beautiful, and vibrant wife. I ignored my role as a husband and now, I am paying the price."

"How old is your daughter, Pastor Wilhelm?" Martha asked.

"Dana is three years old and a few months more. Stupid me . . . I cannot even tell you my own daughter's exact age. She is oblivious to the madness all around us. Understandably, Dana is very close to her mother and her father is a distant thought to her during most days. I would never fight to take her away from her mother. A daughter needs her mother and even though this situation is sin layered upon sin, I am a man who harbors no revenge. The blame lies entirely with me."

Pastor Wilhelm stopped speaking, and he leaned back in the chair and took a deep breath before continuing to speak.

"As I mentioned, I am a complete and dismal failure as a father, husband, and pastor. I want to rip this collar off my neck and never serve as a pastor again, Pastor Paul. How can I ever face my congregation again? The whispers and the humiliation! Valerie and Donny want to begin the divorce processes and they want the baby to be born. They will marry after the divorces. I cannot argue. My beliefs are too strong to condemn an innocent baby conceived in what appears to be true love."

He picked up the shot glass from the table and nervously fingered it in his hands. I thought for a moment that he desired a refill, but he did not ask for one. I then realized that he was searching for words and the strength to say them.

"Consider this my resignation and I wish that I could renounce my ordination and undo my vows. I am a failure. Here, I thought that I was doing God's work and all the time, I was running my life into the ground. Into the ashes of Hell!"

Martha's extraordinary love, her brilliance, and her kindness kicked in and she rose out of her chair, walked over to Pastor Wilhelm, leaned over him, and warmly hugged him.

Martha wiped away a tear and between tears, Martha said, "You are not a failure. Far from it. I am sure your daughter loves you very much. And you are not a fool, either." Martha released Pastor Wilhelm from her hug and slowly stood up. With an abundance of tears in her eyes, Martha proudly stood and said, "You are brave and strong with God's love and to be able to sit here and tell us this wretched story, and admit your own mistakes, proves your worth and your extraordinary strength. Pastor Wilhelm, from the ashes of despair and the fire that turns a glorious wooded forest into dust, wild flowers and small green plants rise and sprout. Then, small trees take roots and slowly, they grow into majestic trees with limbs that touch the tips of Heaven and the limbs absorb the wind, rain, snow, and ice. Birds find new homes in the trees and they build nests within the shelter and inside those nests, birds give birth to new life. Sunlight filters through the trees, and new flowers and plants absorb the rays from Heaven and they bloom in fantastic colors and spread their leaves and roots with the power of hope, joy, and the promise that everything will be better tomorrow."

Martha tugged at the golden chain that held a cross around her neck and she pulled the cross out of her blouse and held it in both of her hands.

While the tears remained on the edges and rims of her eyes, Martha held onto the cross and said, "Yes, everything will be better tomorrow. From the ashes of dust, God recreates life and beauty. Persons such as Pastor Wilhelm recognize the power of ashes and do not allow the despair to drive them down in the pits of Hell. Instead, they recreate, they rise up out of the ashes and become full of new life."

Martha smiled at us; she wiped away her tears and slowly sat down in her chair.

She reached over to the bottle, poured another shot, and mumbled, "After that speech . . . I need another hit of hooch."

I knew why God spoke to my heart.

I loved me some Martha Wiggins.

It was apparent from the look upon Pastor Wilhelm's face that Martha's incredible speech had quickly taken root within his soul. God spoke to all of our hearts during this afternoon and the ashes that fell from the soul of Pastor Wilhelm when he walked into this office, now turned into roots of hope, faith, and beauty.

It was time to release the strong words and thoughts hanging on the tip of my tongue, "I will not accept your resignation. You will not rip your collar off your neck. Instead, you will rise out of the ashes and stand proudly. Ordination is forever. You can renounce it with words from your mouth, but you can never remove it from your heart and soul. Ordination is a part of you. A vow between you and God. You might have become wayward as a father and a husband, but you committed no sins. Yet, perhaps, it is true love and Danny and Valerie found each other. So be it. I will not judge them. God will. Just as Martha said, we now will use the ashes of despair to create something glorious and full of God's glory. We will stand with you and help you through all of this."

With a lean and a tilt in my chair, I asked dear Martha, "Who was the pastor that requested a transfer for any church that ever became available in New York?

Something about being closer to his family. I think he was in Cape May County in New Jersey."

Martha smiled and answered, "Pastor Jonathan Anderson. All Saints Lutheran Church. Cape May, New Jersey."

I smiled and waved in the air for all of us to join our hands together. With all of our hands grasped together in unity, I looked over at Pastor Wilhelm and asked, "Have you ever been to Cape May, New Jersey? Some of the world's greatest beaches. The sand glistens as if there were millions of diamonds lying before your eyes. A historic town, blessed with these glorious, Victorian homes, sandy beaches that stretch from the horizon of Heaven to the very tip of New Jersey, great weather and many pretty women. Besides, they are Jersey gals too! There used to be a beer garden next to a brewery that my brother, Harry and I used to sit in, sip a beer, and watch the sun fall off the face of the Earth. And, furthermore, by order of the Bishop of the Northeast District of our synod, I can assure you that, Fridays and Saturdays for Lutheran pastors stationed in Cape May County, are mandatory days off."

Pastor Wilhelm's smile was priceless.

After a lengthy discussion, we worked out some details and promised to stay in touch. Martha and I sent Pastor Wilhelm off with a lighter heart and a deep acceptance that sometimes God's plan, as well as this crazy life, is full of twists and turns. Once the dust of the visit had settled, I turned my computer on and after it went through the usual gyrations of the blessed reboot, the messenger text window popped up and I leaned in and peered in at it.

"You owe me big time. All that weepy-eyed bullshit has me spinning in emotions. We make a great team. Drinks at the Elusive Lion Pub. On your tab. I love you, Pastor Paul."

I smiled and typed, "We do make a great team. Thank you for you. I love me some Martha Wiggins. Drinks on me. Leave in fifteen minutes. OK?"

The response blinked on my screen like a beacon in the fog.

"YUP!!!!"

Ten months or thereabouts later, after our meeting with Pastor Wilhelm Bruckermann, we received an envelope with a handwritten address on the face of it. Since the return address was from Cape May, New Jersey, then we assumed there was a letter inside, from Pastor Wilhelm. Martha carried it into my office and with some apprehension; she gingerly placed the letter upon my desk. I picked it up and glanced at the envelope as Martha settled into the guest chair in front of my desk. As far as I knew, the transfer between the two pastors had gone along seamlessly and it seemed as if we had worked out a perfect solution to a very difficult situation.

"It is addressed to both of us, dear Martha. Do you want the honors?"

Martha fervently shook her head to indicate that she did not want to open the envelope or read the enclosed letter. I shrugged my shoulders and tore it open. As I pulled the letter out of the envelope and spread it out to read aloud, I saw Martha sink a bit in her chair. Despite her tough exterior, Martha Wiggins was such a softie.

With a nervous cough and a clearing of my throat, I captured my voice from some wayward place and I began to read the letter,

"Dear Martha and Pastor Paul,

Life is full of twists and turns.

Admittedly, I stole that line from a very wise man that I admire very much. I am a bit delinquent in writing and an email seemed to be so impersonal, so I instead decided to send you both this handwritten letter.

If I could thank you both a thousand times, that would still fall short in attempting to capture my gratefulness.

Therefore, I will leave it at that.

The divorces for both Donny and his wife and Valerie and I are finalized. They are free to marry and plan to do so within a month or so. Dana now has a little step brother named Donald Junior. As difficult as this entire situation is and will always be for me, it appears that the baby's conception was within the envelopment of true love. True love is one of God's gifts and it knows no human boundaries. Admittedly, I stole that line from that same aforementioned wise man.

I harbor no resentment; God has grown deep and profound forgiveness in my heart and I wish them nothing but glorious days and happiness. True love hides in very mysterious places. I have been so lucky because, during her pregnancy, Valerie allowed Dana to spend a great deal of time here with me in Cape May. Our reconnecting has been beyond my wildest dreams. In the big picture of life, God only affords us precious little time with our children. In a flash, they are grown off on their own, and leave us with only our love and memories. With God's gift of Grace and love, I realized the errors of my ways and I plan to make the most of every second with my amazing daughter. She makes this life all so real, and Dana fills my soul with joy. Dana loves the beach and I do, too. We swim, laugh, and run barefoot in the sand. We eat endless ice cream cones while walking hand-in-hand down the boardwalk and build giant sandcastles in the glorious sand. Building sandcastles in the sand means more than simply sun, wet sand and surf.

I discovered that sandcastles contain elements of love hidden within their towers of packed diamonds.

I take every Friday and Saturday off. On my days off, I ride my bicycle along the boardwalk and even if Dana is not here with me, I build sandcastles alone on the beach. Practice makes perfect towers! Some days, I stare at sunrises and sunsets and admire God's grandest of creations.

In between, I glorify God.

The church here is wonderful. The congregation is placid and my congregation is abounding with the typical Jersey shore crowd! I have fallen into the flow too and I must admit that this life is easy to love. I am becoming a beach bum! On a recent Friday, I stopped at a brewery that the same very wise man recommended to me, and while I sat in the beer garden and sipped a heavenly brew, I met this glorious woman. Her name is Marjorie, and she is quite beautiful, with long brown hair and sparkling green eyes. Apparently, she looked beyond my frumpiness. We sat together, laughed, chatted, and watched the sun fall off the ends of the Earth. We are taking it very slowly, but on the bright side, Marjorie attended one of our services, listened to me preach, and decided that she still wanted to go out to dinner with me. Time will tell, but in the meantime, I stay the course with God's plan and mission. I have no regrets and I harbor only love in my heart.

I want to detail it correctly. God planted Martha's remarkable words and testimony in my heart and in my mind.

"'From the ashes of despair and the fire that turns a glorious wooded forest into dust, wild flowers and small green plants rise and sprout. Then, small trees take roots and slowly, they grow into majestic trees with limbs that touch the tips of Heaven and the limbs absorb the wind, rain, snow, and ice. Birds find new homes in the trees and they build nests within the shelter and inside those nests, birds give birth to new life. Sunlight filters through the trees, and new flowers and plants absorb the rays from Heaven and they bloom in fantastic colors and spread their leaves and roots with the power of hope, joy, and the promise that everything will be better tomorrow. Yes, everything will be better tomorrow. From the ashes of dust, God recreates life and beauty.'"

"With God standing with me and comforting me, and with both of your combined love, unimaginable faith and your help, and trust, I rose from the ashes. I will continue to do so. Most of all, to the lovely, wise, and amazing, Ms. Martha Wiggins, dear Martha, I promise that, I will submit my budget correctly, because the last thing that I want, is to receive one of those scathing emails!

With all the love gathered from the depths of my heart and with the Grace of our Lord, I love and thank you both.

In the service of our Lord,

Pastor Wilhelm Bruckermann"

I carefully folded the letter and placed it back into the envelope. Martha grabbed a tissue from the ever-present tissue box on my desk. Her nose blowing was loud, and I did my best to suppress a laugh.

"What?" Martha asked between powerful nose blows.

I held my hands up in defense, shrugged my shoulders, and did not answer her. I knew better than to venture into dangerous and precarious waters.

After she dabbed at her eyes to remove the tears and she blew her nose again, Martha leaned in, held her face and nose up at an angle, and asked, "Any lingering boogers?"

Dear Martha had no filter at all.

I leaned in, checked, and said, "No, you are good."

Martha smiled and leaned back in her chair.

She tossed the spent tissue in the trashcan next to my desk and pronounced, "I think that I need comfort food, you know, a big cholesterol-laden-cheeseburger from the pub."

With a nod and a smile, I said, "My comfort food is pizza. Cheese, no extra razz-a-ma-tazz on the top of it. Just gooey, mountains of glorious melted cheese that breaks off in long strings when you bite into it. The kind of pizza that when you fold the slice in half, you need to hold it over the plate and shake the slice until the oil drains off the slice."

Martha nodded and after a long exhale, my faithful assistant made a very profound observation, "Not as good as the promise of joy, and the extra curves added to my ass that the first bite of a cheeseburger delivers, but the pizza lands in second place. I would enjoy a pizza too, and we could help each other with biting off the long strings. It would be fun. Sharing chomps of gooey cheese with you and laughing together as we so often do. Ya know, Pastor Paul, in studying the situation, I think that God created comfort food right after he allowed heartbreak and sadness into the world. After despair arrived, in order to remind us that love exists, God waved his magic creation whoosie in the universe and POOF! Trees, flowers, pristine lakes, golden sunsets, wild sex in the middle of the night, beer and wine, and cheeseburgers and pizza."

"I have to admit that I never heard the creation described in such a way, dear Martha, but it works for me," I answered.

"Hell yeah, it does. More proof that I know my Bible stories. You should allow me to preach one day. That would knock some prudish congregation on their stuffy asses. Give 'em a taste of real life."

I laughed at the mere thought of that event, although I had run across a few congregations in my time that would do well with a taste of Martha Wiggins preaching.

Martha smiled at my laugh and said, "Pastor Paul, we do make a great team. This crazy life is so full of twists and turns. I can say one thing, and that is, I cannot see my life without spending it with you in the service of the Lord. It has been quite the ride. Thank you for you." Martha put her head down and wiped another flow of tears from her eyes and with a quick recovery, Martha suggested, "So, ya wanna hit the pub? All this weepy-eyed bullshit has worn me out."

"Sounds like a plan, and I would not want to even dream of walking this journey without you, dear Martha. We are a great team and God smiles upon our work."

"Hell yeah, we are. That reminds me that I am overdue for a raise. God suggested it to me in a dream. A nice, big, raise. You should not question commands from Heaven, Pastor Paul."

I shook my head and questioned, "In a dream, Martha? Really?"

"Oh well, I might have made the dream part up, but I do deserve a raise."

"I promise to check into it tomorrow. In the meantime, are you still in the need of comfort food?"

"Yup! Okay, the pub it is. No pizza served there, so of course, I win with my choice of comfort food and you will have to wait for the gooey and luscious cheese pizza experience. Not that I am rubbing it in, Pastor Paul."

I shook my head emphatically, trying my best to fake that her winning was the farthest thought from my mind.

"I can wait for the pizza. There is always another adventure, dear Martha. Right around the corner of life."

Martha stood up; she smiled at me and held her hand out. I smiled back and took her warm hand and while still holding hands, we left the office.

I locked the door, and shut off the light and whispered, "Yes, everything will be better tomorrow. From the ashes of dust, God recreates life and beauty. I have to think that in the light of God's power and glory that ashes are severely overrated."

THE END

Letter Five

Beloved Wife,

Shamelessly, I admit that I go through this life with an eye to Heaven. I never take my eye off Heaven. One eye to this world and one eye to Heaven. It works for me. It allows me to cope with the madness. I know that you are there in Heaven and I know that is from where the power and glory to continue my journey arrives to my heart. Every day is a challenge. Every day is another twist and turn, yet I know that with the power and the glory of Heaven pushing me along, I can rise from the darkness. Continually, I write words; I write with emotions that swell from my soul and flood my mind.

I write with a power that gets me through another day. Above all, I write. The words release my emotions, yet they retain my soul.

The previous evening, before writing this short letter, I could not sleep or rest. The night brought too many ghosts and too many memories. I walked outside and looked up at the evening sky. The night was warm; it was still and the sky was wondrously clear. From the edge of the street in front of our townhouse, I could see all the way to the edge of Heaven and a little bit beyond. I knew that you could see me, and you could feel me, and that you could hold me. That is all that I ever need to know.

It is such a great comfort to me.

If I could point at and I could name all the stars in the sky, they all would lead me to you. I could fall upon my knees, roll on the ground, plead for mercy and then rise to my feet, and pray for God to show me my own heart and it would lead me to you.

Always and forever to you.

There is no shame in that fact. In the end, there is only love. Everything else is meaningless dust.

Once again, I go through this life with an eye to Heaven.

I always will.

Love Always,

#27

The Silver Locket

For some weird and strange reason, wandering around stores always stirs up my memories. The only explanation is that I, too, am rather weird and strange! It does not matter the type of store, it could be a department store, a food store, a sporting goods store—it does not matter.

It seems as if the ghosts who constantly haunt me shop there, too.

Even if I have a purpose for shopping, in order to pick up an item for a specific need, I find my mind wandering away from the mission. You would think that I would remain focused, but it is a constant struggle.

Today, there were powerful memories that came over me. Emotional thoughts that ravaged my soul and my mind to recall, yet, in the end, the thoughts provided me with joy in my heart when I revisited them.

I walked by the jewelry counter strategically seated in the center of a large department store. I was on my way to the men's clothing section to pick up some packs of socks and while I cruised past the jewelry department, a glass display case full of women's jewelry caught my eye. Now, mind you, dear reader, I was not in the market to purchase any jewelry for any woman. There was no valid reason for me to allow my eyes to wander there, except for the fact that strange experiences such as this always seem to happen to me. Then, the words flow afterwards as I detail my memories and experiences.

I slowed in my steps and my eyes glanced over the jewelry selection. When my eyes met a display of elegant and graceful gold and silver lockets, then the flow of memories overwhelmed my mind. I found this one particular memory both glorious in content and painful too.

Oh, so glorious and oh so painful.

Since my wife passed, the painful memories rolled over me far too often.

I fought back and sometimes; I won.

Other times, I did not win. They were bittersweet defeats. As of late, it seemed as if every memory had a taste that was bittersweet.

The silver locket sat gracefully on the hints of her remarkable cleavage while clinging to the end of a thin and elegant chain. A chain and locket that exemplified beauty. The chain seemed as if it consisted of tiny threads of precious silver that an angel wove with love and with the power of Heaven. Surely, no human hands could create something so intricate, so tiny, so elegant, and so delicate. On the end of the chain, the locket dangled, held by a single loop of polished silver. The chain was too tiny to glisten very much, but the locket, oh how it glistened. It gloriously glistened and I am not sure that I can find the words or the phrases to describe the appearance. I can try, perhaps, with stars twinkling in a clear evening sky, or perhaps diamonds reflecting sunlight. Surely, they both work as an accurate description, but let me tell you that it glistened like no other piece of jewelry that I ever saw. Sitting there, shining, glistening, and the glowing silver offset with elegant grandeur, the black blouse that she wore so gloriously.

Until now, even though I had met with and spent

countless hours with Maria Tooteroni, and I remain quite sure that Maria often wore the same silver locket during our meetings, I, for some reason, never noticed this amazing piece of jewelry before this meeting. It was strange to me, because I am not sure why I never noticed it, except for the fact that today, my view of Maria was different.

Very different.

Then again, this was a very different Maria Tooteroni and a very different Pastor Paul John Henson.

Ever since a chance and rather weird encounter of what is now many years ago, in a local supermarket where my best friend, Harry M. Redmond Junior and I ran into Maria and her husband Salvatore, while they shopped in a local food store, Maria and Salvatore had been on and off attendees of church services at Reunion Lutheran Church. A church, where I had served for many years as the Senior Pastor before my promotion and assumption of the office of the Bishop of the Northeast District. Although they were members of a local Catholic church, they often felt the need to visit and share in the services at Reunion Lutheran Church. For many years, Maria would make appointments and come in to speak with me in some counseling sessions, where we would speak of religious topics, share scripture, but we would speak of general subjects too. Occasionally, Salvatore would attend our sessions, but most of the time, Maria would come by and visit without her husband. I enjoyed meeting with her. Maria was deeply thoughtful in a wide variety of conversational subjects, both religious and otherwise.

The remarkably wide variety of topics in which her mind would roll through, made me, at times, quite exasperated. She was difficult to keep up with, and to describe Maria as high energy and fast-talking did not even do justice in describing her.

Maria was a very beautiful woman. She had short hair

that she often dyed into wild colors, always vibrant colors such as green, or pink, or blue, and a lean neck and perfect facial bone structure. Her figure was perfect, with generous curves and perfectly shaped breasts. Maria had an engaging and captivating personality, with keen intelligence, and a good sense of humor. She also was rather forthright, and the counseling sessions were, well, how shall we say, at times, rather, "honest" and open in nature. There were not too many subjects of which Maria did not cover, from her wild thoughts after consuming too much red wine on a recent Saturday night, to her past adventures, to her up and down sex life and relationship with her husband . . . it was, at times, a bit difficult!

I enjoyed her company, and I felt as if over the years that I did an acceptable job of assisting Maria with not only her personal issues but also answering her religious questions. Maria and Salvatore never joined Reunion Lutheran Church as full members, but I felt as if they gained from the experience and from our discussions, and somehow, somewhere, they found a comfortable place within their own beliefs.

I had not seen or spoken to either Maria or Salvatore in many years. Time passage was difficult for me to measure because my life often felt as if it was a blur, but my best guess was that I had lost track of them between fifteen and twenty years ago, or thereabouts. Despite my counseling and their best efforts, their marriage always remained a rocky one, and when Salvatore had an offer of a generous promotion and combined the promotion with an opportunity to relocate to California with his employer, they felt as if it was the restart and change that they required for rekindling their relationships and their lives. Salvatore worked in management in a huge retail corporation with stores coast-to-coast and Maria worked as a paralegal. Maria felt as if she could find work anywhere and with her husband given such an outstanding opportunity, Maria was supportive and willing to relocate and leave their lives in New Jersey behind in an effort to begin over once again. If I recalled correctly, Salvatore was from California and his parents and the majority of his family lived there, and that fact was part of the issues in their relationship. In my heart, I felt as if Salvatore suffered with major feelings of homesickness. I never recalled Maria ever mentioning her family. It seemed to be a sore spot and after I brought the subject of her family up in our sessions and was met with a vague answer or a lukewarm response; I decided that Maria had little or no family on her side, or the relationship was strained.

There was always a very special connection between Maria and Pastor Paul John Henson. My beloved Binky told me that Maria had a hopeless crush on me and with that fact in mind, I always remained keenly aware of Binky's observations. I made a supreme effort on my part to manage as best that I could to keep our meetings and conversations strictly on a professional and religious level. There was about fifteen or so years between us, but in all those meetings, the way that Maria spoke so frankly and openly and the way her eyes glanced at me, all combined to convince me that Binky was right on target in her assessment of Maria's feelings.

Now, many years later, it seemed as if the connection remained just as strong. I was quite surprised when I received a phone call in my office a few weeks earlier, and it was Maria Tooteroni not only checking back in to say hello but also requesting if she could stop in and see me again. Of course, it was a voice from the past for me. Now, in looking back on it all, there are so many voices from the past that drift in and out of my experiences and my life that it seems as if it is part of God's mysterious plan for my life. Somehow, Maria had kept track of my life and my career, as well as read many of my books and work. Maria knew of Binky's tragic passing and that of my dear best friend and in fact, as I called him, my brother, Harry M. Redmond Junior, had also passed on and she was keen to the fact that I remained a widower.

Even though we only spoke for a half an hour or so on the telephone, she expressed genuine and deep condolences as to Binky's passing as well as Harry's death too. Maria was always deeply emotional, and she wore her extensive feelings outwardly, as if they were part of her clothing, or, specifically, part of her own body.

On the telephone, Maria could still speak very fast and cover many subjects quickly, but there was something in her voice that seemed very different to me. Maria's voice had deep elements of sadness to it; it was a slightly subdued tone tinged with an element of heaviness. During our telephone call, when I asked about Salvatore, her voice stalled, stopped, and when she spoke again, there was more than just sadness in her voice because there seemed as if there was a vast emptiness to her soul.

For an explanation, Maria only told me, "That is why she was in New Jersey alone and she would explain more when we were able to meet."

It was a Friday in early September.

The prelude to Labor Day.

A special holiday to me because Labor Day had many powerful memories associated with it. The thought of the holiday was wondrously uplifting to my spirit for me to recall the world-famous Labor Day picnics and parties in the Redmond's backyard during my youth, and my teenage years, to my early manhood and to recall the joy of celebrating the good times at good old 20 John Street. Every Labor Day flooded my mind with other memories such as my own family's getaways, to memories of summer romance with the gorgeous and captivating Maureen Zipperelli during a special holiday getaway. Yes indeed, Labor Day always had spectacular memories associated with it for me. It seemed as if it always would be so.

Labor Day, in many ways, is the summer's last hurrah, and in keeping with our usual summer practice, my faithful assistant, Ms. Martha Wiggins, had left work at noon. It still was our summer schedule and Fridays were our "goof-off-days" and our get-away days too. Especially so for the long holiday weekend!

Now, it was just Maria and Pastor Paul John Henson in the office. There was no way for me to know that I was soon to undergo a life-changing experience with Maria.

Life is full of twists and turns.

Maria now sat in front of me, while sitting gracefully in the desk chair in my office in downtown Newark, New Jersey. She wore a black, button-up blouse, open to reveal just enough of her chest to make a man's heart skip a beat or two, and her black dungarees clung to her shapely figure as if they were painted upon her body. Her pants were tighter than tight.

While she had gained a few pounds since we last met, so many years earlier, and her face was fuller and her skin flusher, Maria Tooteroni remained an incredibly attractive woman. For the first time in our many meetings and knowing each other, she did not dye her hair into some extraordinary color. Surprisingly, her hair was a rich and breathtaking black color; with some gentle licks of gray along the edges. Maria now wore her hairstyle a little longer, still on the shorter side, but longer than I recalled, and the black color was what I surmised was her natural hair color. Her brown eyes, somehow, reflected the glow of her face. Brown eyes, almost round in their shape. Usually, brown eyes caused no glowing casts. I am not sure that I was accurate in my description of their influence on me. A glow is the best that I can do.

Maria was truly gorgeous and stunning.

Then there was that amazing silver locket hanging around her neck. A silver locket that, honestly and frankly,

I found difficult not to focus upon, as it not only dangled over the pathway to Maria's glorious breasts but it advertised the silver locket's profound beauty, and in a loud and clear manner, the silver locket broadcasted Maria's beauty too.

Not that either of them required any broadcasting to notice!

After a very warm greeting with many even warmer hugs and some gentle kisses, or two, or three, on our cheeks, we ended our joyous reunion and now, we sat opposite each other and began our discussion and recapturing of so many lost years.

"I must say, Pastor Paul, in fact, no, that is over now," Maria gently shook her head and said, "too many words, too much time, too much pain and way too many lost and crushed dreams. I missed you, I really did. Your quiet insight, your handsome face, your amazing voice and hard New Jersey accent, your quiet wisdom." She then continued, "I mean . . . I am not here for conducting any religious business or for more scripture or Biblical counseling, no, I am here strictly as a friend to catch up for so much lost time, so for the first time, I will simply call you, Paul."

While speaking, Maria nervously fingered the silver locket; she picked it up and then allowed it to drop once again onto her chest.

The ripple that Maria speaking my name caused up and down my spine is still a feeling that, even to this very day, I can feel and recall. It had stirred some intense feelings within my soul. An exciting vibration of some sort that is difficult, in fact, it is impossible for me to define. In my life, only the people closest to me, ever called me by my first name of Paul. Generally, even with those persons, they always called me, Paulie or Pastor Paul, or by my hockey alter ego of my uniform nickname, which became a common label for me as everyone simply called me,

"Twenty-seven." Harry, Rose, my sister, my dear Mum, the old man, and of course, my wife, Binky, would use my first name, but even they often used the other names to address me.

Binky always called me, Paul, in our most precious times together, in moments of passion and in some of our most intimate moments and perhaps, hearing my name whispered from the lips of a gorgeous woman such as Maria Tooteroni was, caused my mind to whirl with the memories and the raw sentiments. It stirred such vibrant and incredible memories and layers of emotions.

Now, I snapped back into reality by the sound of Maria's soft voice, and I realized that the emotions and the ghosts captured me and brought me to a different but a wonderful place. How I wish that these memories did not haunt me as forcibly as they did.

On the other hand, did I?

"Paul? Are you there? That is okay, is it not? Otherwise, if you are uncomfortable, then I will call you, Pastor Paul, and I will. . .."

I cut her off, partly in defense of my spirit, because if she used my name again with that gentle and honestly, sensual voice, then I might break down and sob, and partly because I needed to hide the fact that such a simple whisper of my name had touched me so deeply. We were still so early in this conversation.

"No, please, I am so sorry, Maria. Please, of course, call me, Paul. Thank you."

Maria slowly and gracefully leaned back in the chair and she smiled widely. The silver locket stirred against her chest. She smiled a golden smile full of the elements of the deep depths of her spirit. No doubt, this was a very special woman.

The thought seemed to please her, as if she needed to establish the fact that this was not a meeting for purposes falling within my professional duties, but more as if it was exactly as she defined it to be. This was simply a meeting of two very good friends, in order to catch up on lost time.

"Good. I am so glad. It sounds so wonderful to call you by your first name. Very sexy," Maria said as she giggled.

Her voice came out as a happy, little chortle that came from not her throat, but from deep within her. From the depths of that same spot that produced the golden smile.

"I mean your actual name. It warms my soul and sends chills up and down my spine. A bishop, my goodness it sounds so important."

"Not really. I am just a manager of budgets, real estate, mission work, and pastors and processes."

"Ah, the power and the plan of God are so mysterious. How ironic, the unconventional and reluctant hippie pastor, and former professional hockey player still wearing canvas sneakers and rock-and-roll tee shirts, now moved by the Holy Spirit to be a bishop. The leader. Do you preach very often or conduct any worship services?"

"Very seldom."

"You are still ordained, though, correct?"

"I am. Ordination is for life. In my opinion, it can be renounced but never removed."

Maria nodded and continued, "Interesting. I must say that the years have treated you so remarkably well."

With those words, Maria smiled rather seductively, put her finger to her chin, and pointed her eyes to the ceiling, as if she was deep in thought.

Then Maria's golden voice rolled the words along her tongue, "Age is just a measuring stick, a barometer of some sorts, the true age of a person, lies within their heart, in their soul, and in their mind."

Recognizing the words as my own, I laughed and said, "I see you still have that remarkable memory and that you have been reading my books."

"Of course. Your wonderful books allowed me to own pieces of you, no matter the distance between us. As far as your handsome appearance goes, I really had no doubt that would be the case. You are just as handsome, if not even more handsome, and sexier than you were twenty years or so ago. The long hair, the beard, it all remains the same, if not even better than my memory recalled, just some licks of gray here and there, which only adds even more to your incredible sexiness and smoothness. You do not even have any wrinkles around your eyes. Do you have a time machine hidden away somewhere, Paul? Ha! Look at me. No time machine here. I have wrinkles around the edges of my eyes now. Has it been that long, Paul? I mean, since we have seen each other?"

I thought how in many ways this was still the same Maria Tooteroni that I knew so long ago. She spoke her mind, frankly and openly. I admired that fact. No covers, no dancing around with innuendos. Direct and honest.

"I think it has been at least that long, Maria. All of twenty years. I am very poor at measuring time. No time machine here. Thank you for the compliment. . .."

"Sorry, Paul, but I have to cut you off. Compliment? Really? You can make a woman's heart stop beating!" Maria's eyes blinked a number of times and her mouth turned up on one side in a rather sultry grin. Her eyes then wandered across my face before she spoke once more.

"I must say that your body and build remain amazing too. My goodness, the muscles, as if you still play hockey. In fact, I heard about your involvement in professional hockey. A few more legendary chapters, to add to the ever-growing legend of, Paul John Henson. It was on the news, even in California. I watched that interview on the television with that hot chick host of the entertainment show and watched with some jealousy while she drooled over you. I followed that part of your hockey career with intense interest and I would not even consider myself a hockey fan. Of course, unless the hockey story is about you. Do you still skate and work out?"

"I do. Yes."

"It shows. Most men of your age would die to look as you do. I confess to catching a glimpse of it, so let me say that the rear view is amazing too. Goodness gracious!"

It was not easy to suppress a laugh at the same old Maria, but I did and then said, "Thank you. Okay, well, since we are being so open, you look simply amazing too, Maria. Gorgeous and captivating. Despite your testimony of the lack of a time machine, I swear that you turned back the clocks."

"Oh, Paul," Maria said while grabbing playfully at her mid-section, "look at this flab. You are too kind, but my body has gone wayward as of late. A victim of late-night snacks and munchies while watching old movies alone on the sofa."

Here we go now.

The root of the conversation. No more messing around with compliments or rehashing of the past.

I leaned back in my chair, folded my hands and gently asked, "Alone, dear Maria?"

The golden smile left, and her eyes went down to the floor, then back to my face.

Her glow changed to a frown.

In a low whisper, Maria managed to say, "Yes, Paul. Alone."

I did not answer because I could tell that she had more to say, so I held my thoughts.

"Before I get to that, I have to say once again, even if we discussed it at length on the telephone, how sorry I am about the loss of your wife. To lose a spouse to an accident like that. My goodness and you look so strong and still carry on with your mission. A tower of strength and courage you are, Paul."

She looked away for a few moments while she studied some pictures on the wall of my office, her eyes darting and capturing as Maria caught a glimpse of each of them.

Pictures that were as if they were newsreels of the various phases of my life. Pictures of Binky and me, pictures of Harry and me, and of Rose, and of our children. A picture of the old man, Mum, Dottie, and me. Glorious photos in transparent wooden frames of me playing hockey and of me standing with Bishop Von Houten and Rabbi Goldberg and Father Mark O'Brien. A photo of me preaching in the pulpit on Christmas Eve at Reunion Lutheran Church. Photographs capturing parts and pieces of my life and of all of our lives.

Streetlights along the walkway of life for all of us.

After an inventory of them all, Maria gently said, "And you are a tower of faith."

"Thank you. It was horribly difficult for a long time. Beyond description. I was a mess and even now, I am very good at hiding the pain. Had a bit of practice. You see, my dear Maria, you never get over the loss of loved ones. You just come to some type of cold acceptance. Some type of bizarre understanding of the fact that they are gone. No, no, no, it is not emptiness, which dwells in your heart forever more, and beyond. It is a void of such a deep depth that nothing can ever fill it. Nevertheless, thank you."

"And then, Harry too. What a grand man and a spectacular life lived."

I mouthed another, "Thank you," and then I very softly whispered, "Harry is my brother. Our souls remain forever interlocked. We are never far apart. Ever. The saints in Heaven guard our closeness. Binky and Harry are simply our loss and Heaven's gain."

"Heaven's gain, huh? It is very typical of you to spin such wretched events into some kind of glorifying proclamation to God."

I did not comment, nor did I answer. Maria could tell that I now wanted to hear her sad tale of woe, and the reason she was now in New Jersey without her husband.

Alone. As I was alone too.

Once more, she fingered the silver locket and although Maria's heart was heavy and the golden smile had faded, the silver locket still glistened with overwhelming glory. Her fingers grasped it. She picked it up and then dropped it again while her mind searched for the correct words and her soul grasped at the remnants of whatever remained of her joy.

She, too, was very good at concealing the pain. With a lick of tears in the rims of her beautiful brown eyes, Maria finally spoke, "By the way, my name is no longer, Maria Tooteroni. My name is now, Maria Grace Ellsworth. That is my birth name. Salvatore decided that California's life was very good. In fact, too good. Back in his home stomping grounds, he decided that screwing every available woman and actually, every unavailable, young woman and a few older ones in our neighborhood suited him just fine, well, and good. I, however, apparently, did not make the cut. I guess, as usual, for some reason, I fell short of his expectations. I am never good enough for anyone. Anywhere. Anytime. Thank goodness that we never had any children."

With those words, Maria buried her head in her hands and she sobbed aloud. I immediately jumped up from my chair and walked over to her, knelt down beside her, and consoled her. I wrapped my arms around her and tried my best to absorb her pain. While doing so, I prayed silently in my head for The Lord to help me absorb what had been years and years, and countless events of pain that Maria endured. Bring it all into me, Lord. Let me share her burden, let me hold her pain, and let it cause me to weaken and then be strengthened by you, dear Lord. Strengthened in a testimony to your power and your glory.

"C'mon now, Maria, it is going to be all right. I have you and, more importantly, God holds you tightly in the grasp of Heaven. Let it out."

She sobbed in great gasps of air, heaving uncontrollably

as the pain left her. I felt my prayers answered as I held her tight and the pain left her and entered into my body. It made my knees weak to feel her anguish, but The Lord gave me strength. I gladly accepted her pain and suffering.

After all, Jesus wept.

Jesus felt the anguish, too. It always gave me strength to know that Jesus traveled these same roads too and felt his knees buckle under the weight of despair.

When she caught her breath for a moment or two, she looked up and managed to tell me, "I found him, in our bed, with a neighbor, making love to her in great heaves of passion, after he told me the night before that he was too tired to make love to me. Yet, there he was, in our own bed, with another woman."

More sobs, more pain.

Then a shout of, "I always fall short. I never feel adequate. He told me that I was too much work to love anymore. Too difficult to love. Too much of a project. I was reduced to a project."

I remained stunned that Salvatore would cast aside such a gorgeous, rare, and precious woman, as Maria was. But who the hell knows what goes through certain men's minds? There remained not too much that I could do, besides to hold her and ride this one out. I felt her pain leaving her body. It was something that I had felt many times before, and I determined that it was a gift from God to me, to be able to absorb pain.

Now, I needed to take control of this situation. I could no longer allow the pain to reduce such a perfect woman to a pile of rubble by an incredibly foolish and selfish man's actions and stupid-ass decisions. I gently grasped Maria by her waist and used my considerable strength to coax her out of the chair.

"Okay, I heard enough. I can guess at the rest of this horrible story. Paul can connect the dots on this disaster board. You divorced him, left him to sort out his harem of women, and to choose one woman over the other. How long have you been divorced?"

"About two years or so. Around the same time that I found out about my. . .."

Maria did not finish the sentence, and I sensed that for some reason, I should not pause to allow her to expand upon it, so off I went to finish my supposition.

"Okay, so after struggling for a few years with emotions and life in California, you gave up and came back to where your heart is. You needed to return home to New Jersey. Now, the wretched mess is in the past, in the rear-view mirror of your life and you can begin your life anew, as Maria Grace Ellsworth."

Maria stood up and nodded in approval, and then inexplicably, she strongly nodded her head the opposite way to indicate some type of denial. I was not sure why she did so, but I handed her a tissue from the box of tissues on my desk and she cleaned herself up. Maria wobbled a bit, but I steadied her. Then it might have been the intenseness of the moment, or the reason for the denial, or the pressure of the immenseness of the entire situation, but she looked at me, reached up, grasped my face in both of her hands, and kissed me, long and deep. Honestly, it felt more than glorious, because it felt indescribable.

After kissing me, she buried her head into my chest and said, "Oh, Paul, how I wish that I could tell you how long that I waited for and dreamed about that kiss. A kiss that was beyond glorious but I have to tell you that, no, Paul, unfortunately, I did not return to start over with my life. I finally came home to find you and to find what might be left of me, too. Yet, I have to tell you that there is no starting over, or beginning anew here. I am afraid there is only an ending."

The statement puzzled me, and I was about to ask Maria what she meant when Maria lovingly looked back up at me. Despite her pain and the flow of tears, I studied and admired her beautiful and alluring brown eyes. I felt the glorious beauty that she radiated out of her magnificent body and soul. Maria was beyond gorgeous! My heart felt as if it would jump out of my chest at the sight of her. She blinked her eyes free of tears, but the tears ran from the edges of her eyes and slipped down her cheeks. I took my fingers and gently wiped them away; she reached up with her hands and gently grasped the sides of my face and pulled me towards her glorious lips. I leaned down until our lips met and we kissed once more.

In a gentle whisper Maria said, "Paul, please, I do not want to be alone this long weekend. I have only been in my apartment for a day. I only flew in yesterday morning and I ate in a restaurant and slept in a hotel last evening. Did not want to deal with the mess the movers made when they dropped what is left of my disastrous life on the floors of some lonely and unfamiliar apartment."

Her eyebrows furrowed together in a sign of pain, and then I watched as her eyes darted around as they captured my face.

"Paul, I cannot stand the thought of being alone and now that you are in my arms and I have tasted your love, I cannot endure these upcoming days without you close to me. Not this weekend. No, no, no," Maria said while she shook her head no to state her desire. More tears, her head buried hard into my chest in an effort to hide those same tears, followed by a muted question hinted in more than just the want and need for companionship, but the words danced with desire, "Paul, will you stay with me?"

I looked down and the silver locket glowed with such brilliance that I thought it would damage my eyes.

Instantly, love filled my soul and washed away any of my fears.

Without any hesitation at all, I said, "I will, of course, I will. I will never leave you alone. You are never alone, Maria, you know that God is always there with you."

Maria looked up. She smiled, and with her smile still frozen on her beautiful face and with deeper intentions . . . she powerfully and purposely pulled me tightly into her own body. Very tightly. I could feel every curve of her body and the swell of her breasts and then the resulting increasing hardness of them while they pressed against my chest. I am quite sure that Maria could feel the reactions of parts of my body, too. It had been a bit of time since my body reacted in this way to the touch and feel of a woman.

The emotions of her sobbing began to clear from Maria's voice and in a rather different voice; a voice laced with some huskiness. Maria said, "I know God is always around us and with me. Paul, I did not travel from the left coast to the right coast of America in order to know God. I came to see, and to love, you."

I nodded, kissed the top of her head, and then gently separated from her hug. My thoughts raced and my mind spun, but Maria's well-being was now foremost in my mind.

With great power and fortitude, I managed to ignore the raging in my loins, yet I made no effort to conceal it from Maria. Her eyes darted over my body and focused on certain areas, and I rather easily read her thoughts.

Somehow, I managed to overcome the pounding of my heart and I found the power to speak, "C'mon, let's go and get something to eat. Have you eaten anything today?"

She shook her head, to indicate, no. I took her by the hand and led her out of the office.

"Okay, I have only eaten lightly today, too. We will go. First, we need to eat and have a few drinks and try to relax a bit. We need to chase away some of these ghosts hovering over and howling at the misery. Then, you need to have someone tell you the bloody truth. As my old man said and preached, to tell it as it is. Please, leave your car here. I will drive. We can pick up your car another day. Let's leave everything behind us. After we eat and drink and shake off the ghosts, I need to tell you how glorious you are and more importantly, I need to show you too."

That is what I did. First, I told her that she was rare, precious, and glorious amongst women.

Then, I proved it to her.

Given our past and current circumstances, this evening was inevitable.

When she came to me, later on that same night in her apartment, naked, innocent, exposed and glowing, wearing nothing but that silver locket around her neck, I absorbed her once again. She was beyond gorgeous. In fact, Maria was an immaculate woman.

Flawless in every way.

Yes, her natural hair color was black.

We made love for hours on end.

Once again, I told her that she was rare, precious, and special, too. I told her how beautiful she was inside, and outside, and how she did not make any mistakes; the burden was for Salvatore to weigh. Not Maria.

When we paused for a few moments during our long night of seemingly endless passion, I noticed and then carefully fingered a long scar along her naked back. In the heat of passion, I had felt it on her back, but now I examined it closely. Something inside of me was telling me that this was something important. Even in the dim light of the bedroom, I could see it rather clearly. It was deep and long. Nasty. I held it in my fingers and then gently glided my thumb along the outline of it. I had my share of hockey scars on my body, but this one was different. It was surgical, concentrated, and with a purpose. It was still red and slightly puffy, so I knew that it was an operation that occurred within the last few months or within a year or thereabouts.

"Okay, what is this? Sorry to be abrupt and nosey, but when I touched this scar right now and when we were making love, something tingled inside of me and told me that this was very important."

At first, Maria ignored my question. Instead, she sat up in the bed and quickly turned to me, with the covers and sheets slipping down below her glorious breasts. The silver locket glowing and glistening on her chest. Maria was captivating beyond description. It took very little light to illuminate this stunning piece of jewelry. I now surmised that God illuminated it with the glory of the power contained within Maria's soul. Maria was breathing heavily and her eyes were intent on my body. She ran her hands seductively up and down my chest.

"You are as if a marvelously skilled artist cut a sculpture out of marble. The most remarkable man that I have ever seen, not to mention, having been lucky enough to have shared my love with."

"Maria? You are not answering my question. You are avoiding it and trying to change the subject. Please. . .."

She sighed and then leaned forward, away from me.

I heard her mumble with a slightly shaky voice, "It was a malignant melanoma that surgeons removed out in California about two years ago. I am a New Jersey gal, remember?"

"Ah, huh, yes, of course, the Jersey shore, suntans, and nasty sunburns. Right?"

"Right. Well, it was serious. An aggressive form of skin and tissue cancer. After they carved it out, the doctors made me undergo chemotherapy and waves of tests. It wore me down and made me so ill. It was disgusting."

I sat up and slid closer to her and put my arms around Maria as she explained some more, and in my mind, I replayed the timetable. 'Okay, around two years earlier . . . about the time of the divorce. Geez, my goodness, no wonder she harbors such pain. What Maria had endured was incredible.'

I had to ask to confirm it.

"Correct me if I am wrong, but Salvatore was out of the

picture by now. You went through all of this alone with no support?"

Now, Maria began to weep. Even in the dim light of the bedroom, I could see her tears, so I held her tighter as she wiped them away and nodded to confirm the fact that it was after they divorced.

"How about a church? Did you ever join a church out there? A priest or a pastor?"

"No, Salvatore had it with churches and, as he told me, my ever changing, and wacky ideas on religion. I went to a Lutheran church on occasion, but honestly, without Pastor Paul, it all meant very little. There is only one Paul John Henson. After tonight, I am even surer of that fact."

"Maria, geez, why did you not call your family, or friends, or me?"

Maria then turned and gently pushed me back onto the bed, and when she sensed that I was puzzled, she used a little more force. Maria guided me to rest my head on the pillow, and when I did so, she slid in next to me. Maria placed one hand on my head and ran her fingers through my long hair and her other hand, she ran up and down my bare chest. It was obvious that she did not want to speak with me being able to look into her eyes. Maria and I had spent a huge amount of time together, and she was brilliantly intelligent and conscious of the fact that I focused on a person's eyes during a discussion.

It was an old habit of mine.

While gracefully gliding her hands up and down my chest, she finally mumbled, "Because, I have no family. No real friends. Now, I only have you. I am an orphan. My birth mother was an unwed teenage woman when she gave me life and dropped me off at a Catholic orphanage run by nuns. No one ever adopted me. Instead, I grew up in various foster homes. But no one ever wanted Maria. I know nothing about my mother or my biological father. Nothing, except for this silver locket."

My heart sank, and my mind spun. In all of our time together, all the sessions, all the discussions, Maria never told me, nor did her former husband. Geez, I blew it! It was a major error and an epic failure on my part. I should have probed deeper and asked. Maybe I could have helped more. She never mentioned family, but this was beyond my wildest imagination. An orphan.

She now sat back up and looked down at the locket, and then to me.

"Please, Paul, remove it for me. I want you to see."

I sat up and nodded while Maria spun around and leaned over for me to work the connector on the delicate chain. In the dim light of the bedroom and using my huge fingers, it was not easy to unhook the delicate chain, and I sighed, while I fumbled with the hook. Realizing that it was not easy for me, Maria laughed as I fumbled a bit more with it. It was nice to hear her laugh.

"Sorry, God made me a little oversized. This hook is so tiny."

Her voice changed and in a seductive whisper, Maria said, "Oh, don't, I know it. All parts of you are gloriously oversized."

I did not comment on the actual meaning of her statement, partly because I finally opened the hook and Maria sensed it and she grabbed the locket and chain and held it in her hands. She slid over to the light on the nightstand next to the bed and turned the light on. The light was still dim, the lamp must have been set on the lowest setting, and even though I had just handled every inch of her body, I still admired the fact that her body in the increased light was like the body of a goddess. The sight of her nakedness in the light made me shudder, and as she turned and held the silver locket in her hands for me to take and examine, I felt as if my world was turning over endlessly. If it makes sense, even while sitting in a bed, I was weak in my knees.

God created volcanoes so that every once in a while, they cough up diamonds. In my life, I have been lucky enough to catch some of them and hold them in my hands and close to my heart.

Maria is one of those diamonds.

I took the silver locket and carefully studied it, the power and glory of the piece combined with the significance of it, and it felt as if it exploded in my hands.

"Did you always wear this, Maria? I never noticed it before today?"

"I did, Paul. Well, maybe, because that is all that I have been wearing."

I smiled and said, "No, even before, in the office, when you were, well, you know. . .." Maria finished the sentence for me with a laugh and with the licks of her golden smile. Her incredible humor remained intact.

"Dressed."

"Yes. Dressed. Thank you. I mean, until today, I never noticed it, but when you walked into my office, I saw it right away. I think God opened my eyes to you in a very different way. I think this is all part of the plan. I really do. I mean, we crossed a few questionable lines here today, but love is all around us."

Maria nodded and whispered, "It is. All around us. Obviously, I am fine with all that has happened. It was always my greatest desire. Since we first met. I fell in love with you right away. My goodness, what woman has not? No doubt that I always wanted to feel all of you and to know every inch of you. Of course, years ago, for obvious reasons, I hinted at my feelings and I kept my distance, but my feelings never changed. Now, it is all different for so many reasons, with your situation and mine. There is no reason not to share love. To share and prove my love and feelings for you. Especially right now."

I studied her carefully in the improved light of the bedroom. Maria's eyes were full of love, and she was very confident and determined. Besides, Maria was so matter of fact that this was what should have occurred between us on this day. Yet, for some odd reason, I had no response to her comments. Perhaps it was because I could not argue with her reasoning. No doubt, some lust was involved here, but there was a serious connection between the two of us. A serious connection that existed so long ago and continued to this day. It was undeniable and very real.

Yet, I was not exactly sure of what she meant by the comment of, "Especially right now."

I could not help but to think that there was so much more to this story than loneliness, mutual comfort, and succumbing to attraction and falling into each other's arms in an incredible evening of love and passion. So much more.

"Maria, what do you mean by especially right now?"

Maria deliberately ignored my question and instead, she pointed at the silver locket and said, "Please, Paul, open the locket."

Sensing her intense focus upon the silver locket, I nodded, looked down and gently opened the snaps, and the locket opened, revealing a tiny picture of roses in a garden. Magnificent red roses, framed upon glowing green stems, surrounded by the supporting structure of leaves of hope and joy. Such a tiny picture, yet it was full of detail. I swore that angels must have painted the picture.

"It is captivating. From another world, it is. Who or what we cherish the most in our lives is where we always hide our heart, Maria."

Maria snuggled up closer now. Her bare breasts rested upon my chest, she placed her legs over mine, and her right arm wrapped tightly around me and with the other arm and hand, we held the locket together in our hands.

Maria spoke in a low whisper, full of all the emotion that the world has within it, and gently explained, "I always love your words. Glorious words. My heart is there. Inside of the silver locket. The nuns told me that it was my mother's locket. That my mother wanted me to have it and to know that it was my grandmother's locket before my mother received it. It is the silver locket. The only piece of my family that I know of, Paul. That is all there is to me. I think you are so correct, about hiding our hearts. I think my mother hid her heart inside of that silver locket for me to cherish."

Maria gently placed my hand over the top of hers, and we both held the silver locket in our clasped hands.

"Now, I hide my heart inside of it, too. I used to dye my hair all kinds of wild and different colors and honestly, act a little crazy, in order to hide behind the pain and make myself into someone other than what I am. A disguise. I think that you understand what I mean. You only occasionally reveal hints inside of your mind and unveil parts of your own soul, Paul. Yet, now, I felt your soul inside of me when we finally joined our bodies as one. Generally, you are very private and concealing. I know that when you played hockey, your goalie mask hid the real, Paul John Henson. When you wore it, you became number twenty-seven and no one could find the real, Paul John."

Her insight into my soul and deepest secrets absolutely floored me. There remained profound and glorious reasons that I was making endless love to this remarkable woman tonight.

"I completely understand the disguise part, but as far as this glorious silver locket being all there is of you, no, Maria. You are incorrect. There is so much more to you than just this. Your beauty, your love, your brilliance, and your presence, fills the entire world. Why did you not call me? I would have come out to be with you during all of this."

"Oh, Paul, I almost did a number of times. However, you have had so much in your life. You were lost in a little of your own world of horrible madness. Think about it. All that you had to deal with, I love you too much to have added to your burden."

"Maria, I care and I love. It is my mission. Even before tonight, we shared an awful lot over the years."

"We did. Nevertheless, it is your mission to care for yourself a little too. Besides, it is what it is. I have faith and now, I need to go with the plan. In my heart, I know that tonight is part of that plan. I know that it is. For many reasons."

Once more, the tears returned, and I placed my other hand over hers as we gripped the locket together.

Maria looked up and now, we locked eyes as she said, "And now, you need to know the entire story. The painful truth because I have no shame in saying that you are my one true love. Always and forever. I love you, Paul. More than any words can ever convey. I need to tell you that I am here to not only reunite with you and my soul, but to check into St. Bartholomew's Medical Center to begin more cancer treatments. I check in on Tuesday after the holiday. The cancer is back, and it is in many other parts of my body. The doctors picked it up on a follow-up scan a few weeks ago, before I left California. My prognosis sucks. Very little chance. Even with treatments, maybe, a twenty percent chance to live for three months or so."

Upon hearing her words, with a horrified shock rippling throughout my body, I somehow mustered enough strength to whisper, "So that is the reason for the especially now."

Maria nodded and between tears and in a low whisper Maria answered, "Yes."

That was it for me, now; I worked as hard as I could to hold back the tears. I failed miserably. I grabbed my mop of hair and pushed it all back on my head while my stomach twisted and turned. The room spun in unison with the entire world. The entire world spun, and I could not stop the spinning or hold on any longer. Instead, I reached out and held onto Maria. We held each other tightly and exchanged sobs. As we cried, I replaced the silver locket around her neck.

"That is why I did not want to be alone. That is why I had to be with you, Paul. Just once before I left this world. To honor and prove my love for a real man. A glorious soul, a man, who knows love in his heart, who honors a woman with his love and does not destroy her. It is you, Paul. It will always be you. I needed you to love me just once, for us to be one and to share love, share our bodies and exchange our deepest levels of passion. Just one incredible session of love with you. That is all I ever wanted or needed."

Maria leaned in and once again, she ran her hands gently and seductively up and down my chest while we shared a hard and then a deep and passionate kiss. After kissing, Maria rested her head upon my shoulder while she still ran her hands over every inch of my naked body, exploring and gently touching, as she studied me carefully. We were silent and void of words except that I could hear her breathing change to a low growl that kept time in an alluring rhythm.

Finally, Maria spoke, "Oh, Paul, our age difference means nothing. How I wish, this all could be so different. You are amazing. If I judge our love by the intenseness of our lovemaking, and the level of passion between us, then, I have to say that our love could have been epic and forever. On the other hand, maybe, I should say that *it is* epic and forever because we have these moments to share now and forever in our hearts. I have never had a lover like you, Paul. Never. Even. Close. Your stamina is remarkable. Epic and forever, but I guess the timing was just wrong. Maybe in the next world, my love. Maybe."

"Maria, you are beyond glorious. There are no words to describe you and your love. I love you too, and your love fills my soul with joy. Remember that love is God's greatest gift to us."

Maria smiled her golden smile, but said not a single word. She did not have to speak.

"You hold me in such honor and I am humbled, but I am just a man. A very weak man, who makes many terrible choices. Nothing special."

Suddenly, the world stopped spinning and many strong thoughts resounded very clearly inside of my mind. I knew what I needed to do now.

Rather forcibly, I said, "I need to pray."

I climbed out of bed and dressed.

"Excuse me, Maria."

I left the room, found the door to the hallway just as Maria shut off the light and I heard her soft voice call out, "Do you want to pray together? I can dress and join you."

"No, not right now, Maria. Soon, but not right now. This is between God and Pastor Paul John Henson. The pattern repeats in my life and I need to know why."

In the darkness of the living room of Maria's apartment, I knelt and prayed. To understand, to hope that my faith could and would reveal some type of answer. The answer came back to me as it always does, the same answer, loud and clear. Love her, Paul. Love her as you did Binky, Harry, Sky Blu, Renee, Maureen, and all the others in your life that left you alone. Love them with all of the immense love that I placed into your heart when I allowed you into this world. This time is different, it has to be love of both body and soul. Honor her and extend the faith through the pain. Do not waver and do not give up now. I, your Lord and your God will sustain you, Paul. Now you need to allow Maria to steal your faith and strength. I rose from my knees, returned to the bedroom, and undressed. I climbed back into bed and held Maria tightly.

"Well, Paul?" Maria asked, while sitting up in the bed and carefully studying my eyes. Her beauty, combined with the silver locket's elegance, filled the entire room with glory.

"Paul, what does God tell you to do?"

"To stick with the plan," was my answer. "I will love you with all of my heart, body, soul, and my power. We will cling to our love and to our prayers and hope for healing, together."

Maria said not a word, but she smiled and then kissed me deeply.

A salty kiss, laced with the bitter taste of her tears that flowed and rested upon her lips.

Maria whispered to me between the waves of passion and with tears in her eyes, "Will you always be here, Paul? Just as you have always been for me?"

"I will always be here. In the dark and in the light. The happy times and the sad times, the desperate times, always and forever, I am always here. God will not allow me to be anywhere else."

Maria smiled and off we went to a very special and unique place.

During that long, yet overtly short, holiday weekend, we only stopped making love to shower together, to eat and drink and to walk to the corner store in order to pick up supplies of wine, beer, and some snacks. At times, it became so hot in that apartment's bedroom that it is a wonder that the paint and wallpaper did not peel off the bloody walls.

We ordered a helluva lot of pizza too.

I stood in the corner of a hospital room in St. Bartholomew's Medical Center in my old home city of Paterson, New Jersey. It was a much-respected hospital. I kept telling myself that fact. As if I felt that the doctors and nurses here could overcome God's plan through their skills and tools.

A medical procedural expert sat in a chair and she explained the plan and procedures, while a nurse prepared Maria for chemotherapy treatments.

The woman, who was explaining the treatment plan, finished with her explanation of the treatments. She then paused and studied me.

Our eyes met for what seemed to be a long time and the woman asked me, "Are you the emergency contact for Maria, Pastor Paul?"

"I am."

"Oh, okay, got it. Please, her next of kin, can you help me with that?"

"I can, it is me."

The worker looked up from over her glasses at me and nodded her head while she took some notes. I glanced over and watched Maria grimace as the nurse poked an I.V. needle into her arm.

Now, the horror begins. Lord, give us strength.

"You are obviously her pastor, so we have her religion as Lutheran."

"No, I am not her pastor, but Lutheran is correct. Yes, it is." I leaned in, glanced at the medical worker's name tag, and caught her name. "Honestly, since you are all sworn by medical secrecy rules and laws these days, Ms. Davison, I am Maria's best friend and I am her lover. I love her with all of my body, heart, and soul."

Ms. Davison dropped her papers and her pen on the floor. The nurse's head spun around, and the nurse's eyes stared long and hard at me. I watched her eyes go from my pastor's collar around my neck, to my black suit, to the wooden cross hanging by a lanyard around my neck, to my beard and long hair. Her eyes studied my fingers for rings and seeing none, she smiled, as did Maria, who, despite the pain in her arm, gloriously laughed at the immenseness of the situation.

The nurse looked at me again, then to Maria.

The nurse then said to Maria, "Hoowee. My goodness, girl, you are one lucky gal. I need to take your temperature and I might need to take mine too. That man is hotter than seventeen Hells."

Maria winked at me and smiled that golden smile. The silver locket never shone so brilliantly.

"He is. No doubt that he is. I am lucky. I really, really am. The luckiest woman in the entire world because God's greatest gift to us is love."

I smiled back at Maria and proudly announced, "Love *is* the greatest gift. And, no, I am the lucky one here. I am a lucky man in so many ways because Maria is beyond beautiful. Her beauty is beyond words to describe. Maria is gorgeous, inside and outside too and she fills my heart and this world with love and with joy."

Maria never left St. Bartholomew's Medical Center alive. It was not part of the plan. Despite the aggressive treatments, the cancer was too powerful, too far spread. At the end of three months, it ravaged poor Maria. She withered before my eyes from a vibrant woman into emaciation. Her hair fell out, and she vomited blood every day. Enough of this! I cried to The Lord for mercy and pleaded with The Lord to stop the agony. My heart was breaking into so many pieces that I was not sure that I could gather the strength to watch and endure this wretchedness any longer.

Maria decided to end all the treatments and enter into hospice care. Despite the pain and the agony, her gorgeous beauty remained.

Beauty, inside and outside, beauty beyond words or comprehension.

I visited her every day and every night. Often, twice a day and even more. Due to my clergyman's status and not because we were lovers, the night-shift nurses allowed some bending of the rules and looked the other way, while I spent every night in a chair next to her side.

Endless tears and painful discussions. Precious little time we had together.

So precious.

Maria was very brave, full of love, and full of faith. Truly, she *is* an amazing woman.

Maria desired cremation and to have her ashes spread in the ocean at the Jersey shore. She was quite specific and adamant and made me promise that there would be no notification to Salvatore. None whatsoever. She donated all of her worldly possessions to Lutheran Social Services.

However, the silver locket was forever my own silver locket to keep. On the day she asked for hospice care, Maria gently placed it in my hand and closed my fingers around it while kissing me very deeply.

I planned to give it to our granddaughter, when and if she marries or upon my passing away, it will be in my will for her to receive it. My son-in-law adopted our granddaughter after her biological father abandoned her and signed her adoption papers over to my daughter and her second husband. Considering the circumstances of her life and of Maria's life, it seemed to be an appropriate gift. Until then, the silver locket will remain safely locked within my safe.

Heed my warning, with all my power and honor and my swearing to both Heaven and Earth, that I will guard the silver locket with my own life.

The day before Maria slipped into a doctor administered pain medication-induced coma to relieve her terrible pain; I brought to her three dozen red roses and placed the roses in a huge vase right next to her bed. She loved them and we compared the roses in the vase to the picture in the silver locket. I held her hand all day and all night, too. I stayed next to her bedside, managed to stay awake with God's help, and I read scripture aloud and prayed the entire night. The next morning, all that remained were closed eyes and a slow but relaxed breathing. But thankfully, the pain and suffering were over. After I lost my wife, and I fell into the depths of ruin and finally crawled back to this world, I vowed and made a promise to my loved ones, and most importantly, to dear Rose that I would never allow grief to overcome me ever again and allow the defeat of grief to invade my soul. Grief tramples life and it drowns out the happiness and glories of love. Yet, with God's Grace, love overcomes all the pain. Grief was not going to win this one. I kept my vow when Harry left us, and I intended to keep my vow now. Maria was full of life and love and nothing would trample that in my heart.

Maria passed away three days later, on a glorious day full of sunshine and gentle breezes. One deep breath and then she was gone from me and from this world. I felt her love fill my soul as I held her hand during her last breath.

I swear the scent of those magnificent roses surrounded me as if they were a cloud of testimony of her love when she passed.

Heaven's gain.

Alone, standing on the sand, I spread her ashes into the ocean at the Jersey shore on a day very similar to the day in which she entered Heaven. With a gentle prayer and a kiss on my lips, I tossed three dozen red roses into the waves; I stood there and watched the waves carry them to and from the shore. Waves of emotions, filled with love and red roses, and Maria too. I held the silver locket in my hand and honestly, the glory of the silver locket filled the entire world and I was quite sure that the locket's radiance crept into Heaven, too.

"Can I interest you in purchasing one of our gold or silver lockets, sir? They are all on sale today. I can give you a wonderful deal on a special gift for that special woman in your life."

A very attractive saleswoman with long red hair and a wonderful smile spoke to me, and her voice snapped me back to reality. I felt like an idiot because I had no idea how long that I had zoned out in front of the sales display.

"I am sure such a handsome and stunning man as what you are, has a very special woman in his life."

Ah yes, a little touch of charm along with the sales pitch. Hey, everyone has to make a living.

"Oh yes, thank you, but I was just browsing. I actually have a fabulous silver locket already. It is full of love and glory. Someday, I am going to give it to our granddaughter as a very special gift."

"Oh, okay, then your wife and you have shared it, and you have a plan. I guess."

I shook my head and said, "Well, no. It was actually a very special person's possession. She willed it to me. I am a widower. My wife passed away a long time ago."

I thought how it was silly to reveal so much information to a sales person. The emotions rolled over me and made my mouth too loose. Oh well.

"Oh, I am very sorry to hear of your loss. Well, if you change your mind, here they all are. Besides . . . I am here too," she said with a wink and smile.

I waved and thanked her and walked away. I took a few steps, then stopped and turned and returned to the sales counter.

The sales woman seemed surprised at my speedy return. She looked over at me, smiled and said, "Wow! That was a fast change of your mind. I would like to think that it was my wonderful sales pitch or my pretty smile."

"Both. Say, which one of these silver lockets is your favorite? I mean, which one, would you wear? I am not too swift at this kind of shopping."

I smiled and pushed all my long hair out of the way while I leaned over and stared at the sales display.

"Oh, well, that is easy. This one. The one with the diamonds. The most expensive one, of course. A piece of advice, handsome man, you should never ask a woman for her favorite. It will always be the most expensive one."

No mirror handy, but I am sure my face grew very intense.

The passion rose in my soul and it reflected in my words, "I guess, but money does not really matter. Does it actually matter? Am I incorrect? In the end, what does it matter? Only love really matters. Love is God's greatest gift to us. When everything is dust, only love remains. The money becomes the dust sifting through the fingers on our hands."

I watched her face break into a slight smile, and her eyes studied me. Her eyes went from my eyes, to my long hair, to my beard, to my face, to my faded rock-and-roll tee shirt, to my black dungarees, to my canvas sneakers. I am sure she had no idea that I was a Lutheran bishop. Maybe some wayward hippie, but never a clergyman.

With intention, I broke the spell and asked, "Say, how many of these exact silver lockets do you have in stock?"

"Ah, ah, okay . . . I will need to check in the stockroom and yes, I agree with you about money and love. Honestly, your words caused my spine to tingle. They went right through me and for a few seconds, I could not speak. I needed to regain my thoughts and, honestly, my soul. My soul almost escaped with your words." She paused, shook her head, and breathed very deeply before continuing. "Anyway, thank you for those glorious words and amazing thoughts. Please wait. I will be right back."

I watched her disappear behind a wall and within a few minutes, she returned holding jewelry boxes.

"Handsome man, I have four and the one on display."

"Good. In fact, perfect."

I quickly figured it in my mind—one for Rose, one for Heather Sarah, one for Blue Cloud, one for Dottie, and an extra one.

"I will take all of them. Please gift wrap them and keep one for you."

She almost dropped the boxes, and I laughed.

"Please, tell your manager to come over here and I will explain it. I mean—do you want one?"

She smiled and said, "Of course, but it is very strange and I am sure that it is not really allowed."

"As I said, I will explain it to your boss. Please ask the manager to come see me and I will work the deal. I am from the north side of Paterson in New Jersey and I am very good at working out deals."

"Well, okay, but this is kind of amazing. Shocking! This is a six-hundred-dollar locket. You are a special man and I have to ask. Are you going to ask me out on a date? I am available and I assure you that I am not married or dating anyone seriously right now."

I laughed and said, "I am hardly special at all. Just a man. A man who simply wants to honor someone that filled this world and my heart with love. That is all."

"Oh, yes, the original owner of your silver locket. The person who gave it to you. I understand. How wonderful of you, she must have been special."

"Yes, incredibly so. Beyond words."

"Ah, about the date?"

"No, sorry. Nothing personal. But, please know that you are gorgeous, inside and outside too."

"Oh, too bad, because I would go out with you in a second." She extended her hand and said, "Anyway, thank you for an amazing gift from an amazing man. My name is Claire Dawson."

I shook her hand and said, "You are welcome, Claire. I am Paul John Henson. Thank you."

For some reason, of which I was not immediately sure of why, I left off the pastor title, and certainly, I left off the bishop title to my name and introduction. After some pause, I think that I wanted to leave this all here on Earth and exclude the power and the glory of Heaven. I think that sometimes, God expects us to take up the mantle on our own.

After explaining the purchase to the perplexed and dazed store manager and receiving strange looks and eventual approval, as well as a covert slip of the sales woman's telephone number written on a small piece of paper, "In case that I changed my mind," I walked away with the gifts in my hands, wearing a terrifically broad smile.

I recalled that I still needed to pick out the socks. Oh well, the hell with them.

My thoughts overwhelmed me.

It felt so good.

I felt renewed.

Yes indeed, renewed once again.

While I joyfully exited out the store, I spoke aloud, "I will always be here. In the dark and in the light. The happy times and the sad times, the desperate times, always and forever, I am always here. God will not allow me to be anywhere else."

THE END

Letter Six

Beloved Wife,

I know that we discussed it many times and as painful a subject as it was, we always agreed that if one of us left this world and went first to reside in Heaven that, if the person was the right person, we would allow ourselves to fall in love again. I am comfortable with that discussion because I know that for one of us to neglect God's incredible gift of love, is incredibly misguided.

For a long time, I struggled with this raw emotion. I now fully understood Harry's struggles with loving anew after Sky Blu left us.

The thoughts and emotions caused me such guilt. Yet God steers me. God steers me all the time and often I disagree with the control God has over me. Oftentimes, as unwilling as I am to go in the various directions that God leads me, I do eventually follow the plan.

Whatever the plan might be.

I am not sure if I follow the right path because I seem to make so many errors, commit some sins, and stumble with some obviously glaring mistakes.

It was not until you were gone that I realized how much I relied upon your amazing mind and your brilliant guidance. Now, I often spin in the wind. Luckily, I was smart enough and lucky enough to have Rose in my life to straighten me out and put me back on course.

It is so different now.

A different world, but the memories of what we shared, remains strong and powerful. They never leave me alone. I jump out of bed in the middle of the night, arisen from a deep sleep, from within an encompassing dream. A time from so long ago and I sit straight up in bed thinking that I hear your voice calling me. Rose steadies me and calms me with her touch, with her love, and with her quiet power. Rose holds me tightly in her love and in her soul. I thank God for her, all we have, and all we share. I love Rose dearly, boldly and completely. Our passion fills my life and our nights with love.

I know that you understand.

I pray that you do.

Between the daily comings and goings of what has been a busy retirement life for us, I continue to write and detail past events. Some of my recent work has some of my romantic adventures that occurred after you left us contained within them.

Don't worry. I am leaving the super-steamy stuff out.

I can see you looking over my shoulder, fluffing your long hair, digging your left foot firmly into the floor and then advising, "Tell the true story, dear twenty-seven, but please keep it tasteful, yet, emotional and do not you ever dare to write about our love life. The devil will be in those details, Paul. No secrets, now."

Ha! Yes, indeed, I can see you standing right next to me saying that while watching as I type.

I am not sure why I have recalled some of those parts of my life and why I feel the need to write about it, other than they are parts of my life that contain such intense and raw emotions and after all, these are the Chronicles of Henson.

I guess that is a valid reason. I hope that I am not reducing my inspiration to begin writing such literary wonderment as composing some dramatic, dime-store romance novels. My goodness!

Oh well, I simply write what comes into my mind. I am not selective, nor do I write within any specific guidelines or genre. It is a simple process for me, because I ponder the subjects, I recall the adventures and details and then I write the chronicles as they enter into my mind.

Honestly, I am not surprised, given the recent past years of our lives, that much of this material has such a deep and dark vibe to it. The last few years have been difficult to endure, and it seems as if at the end of my career, God sent me an awful lot of difficult situations to handle, to deal with, and to resolve. It was a good test of my spirit. A test after my recovery from grief, a test to make sure that I was following God's plan. I think that it makes some type of sense.

Does that make any sense, dear Binky?

I hope you think it does and I hope that you understand that not all the writings can be humor-filled or laced with the wackiness of our adventures. Some stories can have the humor and the wackiness, yes indeed, but not all, and there are so many more to detail. Onward the adventures continue to march into my mind, and often, I feel as if I have only barely touched upon some of them.

Seemingly endless they are.

Right for now, I am not sure if I will run out of words, events, or if I will run out of time. It is now a race between God's intentions and Paul John Henson's words to see which one occurs first.

Until then, I will write on.

Love Always,

#27

Layers of Emotions

My goodness, sometimes the ideas just run up into one another. Too many adventures, too much to recall. I tried keeping a small notebook with me to jot down ideas, conversations and notes of persons that I meet along the way and for a long time, it worked. It worked until the notebook was so full of random notes and stupid-ass ideas that I could no longer decipher it or make heads or tails of what I had written. It became, much as my life had become, a blur of words and experiences. Lately, I wished that I were a victim of the dreaded, "Writer's Block."

Alas, I am not.

In fact, it is quite the opposite, because I am a victim of "Writer's Deluge."

I think that I just made that term up.

Dear reader, I am hoping that you understand that the words, events, and experiences come so hard and so fast that I cannot put them into words on these pages quickly enough.

My goodness!

On a recent Saturday evening, I paced the floor of my home office and tried my best to sort it all out and decide which stories and words should come first. A nagging memory of long ago would not let go of me, but I could not tell where the memory was leading me. After pacing for a solid fifteen minutes, I sat in the comfortable leather chair behind my amazing writing desk in my office in our townhouse. When we bought this home, our daughter, Heather Sarah, purchased the furniture and decorated the office for me. Memories surrounded me here, pictures on the wall, hockey memorabilia, and on the far side of my office, sat my first writing desk that Binky and I bought and tucked neatly in the corner of our small rental home in Great Falls, New Jersey. I was not short of inspiration, that was for sure.

Oh yes, we also have the custom designed and built and expertly installed wet-bar that Heather Sarah insisted that I have constructed for my office. The wet-bar sat along the longest office wall, fully stocked with all our favorite selections of beer, wine and liquor, and it even had these really cool, small, blue-colored L.E.D. lights installed in and around the shelves that cast this glow of allure on all the different colors of the bottles on the shelves. I use the lights as mood lights and often find myself staring at their soothing glow. When not in use, the wet-bar neatly hid behind sliding oak doors. I looked at the two fingers of Scotch sitting in my glass on the desk and then to the wet-bar. The oak doors were open tonight. A small sip of the Scotch rolled across my tongue, and then smoothly glided down my throat. The liquid numbed my mind, but it also worked some magic on my insides.

The door to my office was open, and I heard the gentle pad of Rose's feet in the hallway and her soft voice called out, "You doing okay in there, Paul? I assume you are still working on some masterpiece. I am going to take a shower now. The movie is over. You did not miss much. Once more, the reviewers have their brains somewhere where the sun does not shine. It was not even so, so."

Rose appeared in the doorway and smiled that gorgeous smile of hers. I looked up and smiled back. Our love filled the entire world. My wife is amazing both inside and outside. I leaned back and nodded. Rose posed in the doorway of the office and carefully studied me. Her dazzling smile, the ever-present, small golden hoop earrings in her ears caught the light of my office, and while she moved her head, the earrings glowed with seduction. Rose wore one of my old hockey sweaters and I am quite sure there was nothing underneath it. Rose loved to wear my hockey jerseys.

"They smell like you do and are soooo comfortable," Rose often told me as she selected which team and era she wanted to wear. It was a fact that she had more hockey sweaters on her side of the master closet, then what I did on my side.

"You have a dazed look in your eyes, Paul. Either too much Scotch or not enough Scotch. Not sure which it is. Or you are stalled somewhere in your work."

"Stalled, my lovely Rose. I cannot decide where to go with these few opening lines. Too many ideas and no clear direction."

Upon hearing my testimony, Rose nodded and then walked into the office and without saying a word, she walked over to my desk, picked up my glass, and then she walked over to the wet-bar. When she arrived at the bar and reached up to pull the Scotch bottle off the shelf, the hockey jersey slipped up and the glorious view revealed to me what I already knew. As I said, Rose was a gorgeous woman, her figure improved every day.

"Why do you keep this bottle up so high? You are six-foot gazillion, or whatever the hell you are, and I am six inches tall. Why do you do this to me?"

I leaned forward for a clearer and closer look at the amazing display and laughed as Rose realized that her bare backside was fully exposed. Rose reached behind her and touched her glorious, bare backside. Now, I was laughing so hard that I began to lose my breath and Rose began to laugh, too.

"Oh, I get it, so you can check out my bare ass."

"Yup. An evil plan of mine that worked perfectly."

When you have a lover and a soul mate that you can smile and laugh with every day, then you have found one of the keys to the Gates of Heaven.

While pouring some more whiskey into the glass, Rose said, "Well, you do not need an evil plan to see me in my glory. Anytime, anyplace, anywhere. Around you, my clothes melt off my body. Here is some liquid inspiration," Rose said, while she walked to the side of my desk and set the replenished Scotch glass down in front of me.

"Thank you for the glorious view and the refill, Rose."

With a nod, Rose said, "I would invite you in the shower with me, but we would, as the old man would have said, 'swap spits' and with this head cold that I feel coming on, I would not want to risk sharing it with you."

I picked up the drink and took a little sip while lifting my eyebrows rapidly up and down in jest and saying, "It will be worth it. It always is."

"No, it won't. You only say that now in waves of lust, but in two days when we collapse together in bed, surrounded by aspirin bottles and waves of menthol, sneezing goo and slobbering all over each other, then you will regret it."

Rose waved her hand in the air at me and smiled.

"Instead, I will suffer on my own and leave you to write like a mad demon. I would use a harsher term that you will write like a blankety-blank but that is an inappropriate and obscene statement to make for my now, retired, pastor, slash, husband, and for me, as a woman of faith to say."

I laughed again and set my head back and when I did so, I spotted the date on the calendar on my office wall. For some reason, I took notice of the date. It was the last week in May. Almost exactly two years to the very date that I proposed marriage to Rose.

Suddenly, the memory and direction hit my mind like a hockey puck, smacking into my head. What Rose just said, first, quoting a favorite saying from the old man, and then mentioning writing like a blankety-blank, combined with the date, and it all shook loose for me.

Rose saw the change in my face as I leaned in close over the screen of the laptop and mumbled, "A bit of an obscene statement, yes, but it would be wonderfully accurate." I then looked up at Rose and said louder, "I love you to the moon and back, Rose. Maybe even farther."

"Oh, oh, I saw the inspiration arrive on your face, Paul. I love you to the same place. Off to my shower I go, all alone except for my runny nose and quickly closing off sinus passages. I go with all of my love and one last tease of inspiration."

With one quick motion, Rose pulled the hockey jersey off and over her head. She tossed it over to the desk, and I grabbed it out of the air. She posed and winked, and I felt my loins ache at the sight of her.

"Good catch, twenty-seven. You thought the other view was nice, well, here, you go. That will teach you to put the Scotch bottle up so high. I will see, and enjoy, all those glorious parts of you in, ah, what do the doctors say? Ah, seven to ten days. You should be good and blue by then."

I watched Rose's naked glory sway and weave as she disappeared into the hallway and beyond.

I yelled out to Rose, "You are going to catch even more cold walking around all bare ass like that!"

A very faint, "Ha!" was all I heard.

What a woman! The lovely Rose.

Recovering from that glorious interlude, I went back to work. Now, the memories and ideas were all around me, and I felt my fingers shaking as I went to type on my trusty old keyboard. Okay, here we go, I have it now, late May, write like a mad demon, an old man saying.

"Write on."

The layers of emotions that welled up inside of me today while I walked the few short, city blocks through downtown Newark, New Jersey to the Office of the Bishop of the Northeast District remained impossible to describe. The thoughts ran rampant throughout my mind. These walks to the office along these city streets were going to be counting down now. The daily walks to and from the office. I did not know exactly how many more times that I would make this journey, but after what transpired over the past few days and the weekend, there remained little doubt that it was counting down. So much had happened since last week that it was difficult to imagine how my life could so quickly change. You would think that by now, I would honor my own saying of, "Life is full of twists and turns." A simple walk down a street that I walked a thousand times before now invoked such layers of emotions. My goodness, what a softie I was.

Harry was so correct when he said that, "I was an old lady."

I laughed aloud as I came to the first intersection and waited for the "DON'T WALK" sign to indicate that large groups of "City Walkers" were free to walk once more. I laughed, because I recalled how my faithful and long-time assistant Ms. Martha Wiggins despised the walk to the office. My laughing aloud at Martha's antics and colorful descriptions caught the glare of a crabby-faced, middle-aged woman. The woman had dyed red hair in a slightly subdued hue that matched her own subdued demeanor. Ms. Crabby sipped a container of coffee, in a manner similar to how a baby sucks on a pacifier. She first looked at me, then at my long hair, my beard, and then her gaze moved to my black suit and pastor's collar and she frowned. Ms. Crabby took another sip of coffee. I imagined that she was anti-religion as well as, to a certain extent, anti-happiness.

I smiled and said, "Good morning."

She ignored me and looked back to the sign that ruled our lives.

"Well, pardon me for interrupting your world with a laugh," I mumbled just loud enough for her to hear.

The light finally flipped to "WALK" and waves of humanity stepped off the sidewalk and moved across the intersection. Three more city blocks to go.

Anyway, as I mentioned, Martha was my longtime faithful and marvelous assistant. She was famous for her forthright ways, and her rather honest and "unfiltered" manner of speaking, as well as her reputation for being rather tough. We worked together for many years at Reunion Lutheran Church, and when I received the promotion to the Office of Bishop of the Northeast Lutheran District, I asked Martha to join me here in the same role. Martha was part of our family. She remained with me through thick and thin, through tears, through stress, through the happy times and the bitter times and the agony. We shared our lives together. Honestly, I would not know what to do without her. If someone asked me how long Martha and I have worked together, surprisingly, I would fail to be able to provide an accurate answer to the question. Suffice it to say that it was forever.

If someone asked Martha, she would roll her eyes and answer, "Too damn long."

At first, when I took the position of bishop, Martha complained fervently about how the parking here in downtown Newark, "Royally sucks. It costs a damn fortune. I would be better off flipping burgers by the time that I pay for a lousy parking space in some stupid-ass parking garage that no matter when I arrive, only ever has open spaces on the top level. It is too far away. What the hell? Really? I mean, c'mon now, nine levels of a parking garage high! All the car fumes of the city are stuck up there. Right in the spot where I park my car. Plus, the parking space is so small that an ant's ass can't fit in it."

While I did not describe the parking situation in quite the same colorful manner as did dear Martha, I had to agree with her assessment. The office tower that we rented office space in had a huge parking garage that was about two blocks away from the building, and it did cost quite a bit of money to park there. All urban cities have the same parking issues. In the locations where Martha and I live, mass transit really did not cover the areas too well and the lack of mass transit made driving your car into the city a necessity. After months of Martha wearing my ears out and then one day, her dragging me out of the office and out to her brand-new car to show me the dent she received in her door, I resolved to arrange an improved parking situation for Martha and me.

I also paid for the repair of her dent.

Having inherited deal making from my roots in the old neighborhood where deal making was a subject taught in second grade, right before math and after social studies, I found a cigar chewing, slightly greasy, baldheaded guy of Italian heritage named Franco, who owned a small building that housed a number of storefronts in it. I worked a deal out with Franco and for a small sum of dough; he allowed Martha and me to park in his small parking lot. Like some shady crook paying off bets on the horse races, I paid Franco a few dollars every Friday. I placed the dough in an envelope and slipped it under a creaky wooden door in the rear of the building. For years and years, I slipped envelopes under doors, and now that Franco Senior is retired and living in Florida, I slip the money under the door for Franco Junior.

Franco Junior is greasy, baldheaded and chews cigars, too. With the money, I paid for parking two vehicles for over twenty years or whatever it is; I could have bought a parking lot for Martha and me.

The "Franco" parking lot was four city blocks away from the office. *Short* city blocks.

Martha still was unhappy. According to Martha, Franco's parking (as we called it) was in Australia. The parking garage was two *long* city blocks away, not including the walk across the parking level, then down the elevator, across the other level and then out onto the city sidewalks.

One snowy winter's day was the final straw when she complained, "I froze my ass off walking here today." Martha added, "That Franco's was only better than the rip-off parking garage because Franco washes her car once a week, cuz he has the hots for me, and that there were no more dents on her car. It's still all the way in Australia!"

Now it was my mission in life to prove dear Martha wrong. I should have known better. Her husband, Bradley, warned me years and years ago that Martha Wiggins was never wrong.

I bought a pedometer and Martha and I bet beers at "The Elusive Lion Pub" that Franco's was closer than the garage was.

One day, together, we paced off the distance and allowed the pedometer to measure the steps. I won and Martha still made me buy the beers.

"Well, you have to pay because I hate them damn 'WALK' and 'DON'T WALK' signs. They remind me of my husband telling me what to do."

I loved me some Martha Wiggins.

She was one of a kind.

My progression down the city street and through my thoughts and memories brought me to the next street corner. I found myself in and amongst the waves of City Walkers standing on the sidewalk waiting for the stupid-ass "WALK" sign to change. Ms. Crabby was next to me again, and she still sucked on her coffee and had that look on her face as the old man would say, "It looks like she is sniffing, a load of cow manure."

The words of the old man ran over me and once again, I

laughed aloud and she glared at me.

I stole another one of the old man's sayings and mumbled, "Crab-ass" as the demon known as the pedestrian control light changed to "WALK" and we all rolled off to the next block. An elderly man walking in front of me struggled a bit with the walk and stepping onto the curb. The traffic light changed from red to green, and the horns blared and fists shook because this is New Jersey and the old chap was, "In the way." I stuck my arm out, assisted the old chap back out of danger, and made sure he was safe on the sidewalk.

"You okay, sir?" I asked.

He smiled, nodded, and said, "Thanks, father. I am just old and wobbly, and forgive me but, those drivers need to have their horns stuck up their asses."

"No forgiveness required because I agree and so does God."

I did not correct his incorrect title of addressing me as father. People often mistook me for a priest or a monk. What does it really matter? In my opinion, it is all the same. I watched the man wobble and totter on his way and another "old man moment" spun into my mind.

My old man just had an uncanny knack for perfectly capturing certain general aspects of this strange thing we all call life. My father could capture an image of a certain person, place, or thing so perfectly with a curt description or a short phrase or even a word or two. Often, it was perceived to be a smug remark, or critical, but once you understood the "Old Man Speak" dialect, then you realized that he was just being, well, for lack of any other description, the old man. However, his descriptions were dead on target.

When he was old and growing feeble, and the onset of that wretched Alzheimer's disease began its evil grip on him, he had a major trouble with walking. His walk grew to be more of a painful shuffle of his legs.

The old man, in using his uncanny knack, called his shuffle, "Wobble Ass."

Our dear Mum would laugh and then, as she usually did, she tried her best at cleaning up the "Old Man Speak." Mum would also remain honorable to her English heritage and put her own special twist on the phrase.

Mum would say in her best English twist, "You are a little wobbly fobbly, dear Paul."

The old man would look at her, shake his head, and proclaim, "What the hell does that mean? English bullshit. I am, Wobble Ass."

He then would continue wobbling along on his way. I mean, I am sorry; he would, "Wobble Ass" along on his way.

His trouble with walking was one aspect of his aging that I struggled greatly with, because not only had my father been a terrific baseball player and an excellent track and field runner, but also some of my fondest memories of my youth were of walking with my father on the sidewalks of the city streets around our old neighborhood. Just as I am walking today and allowing these memories to run ramshackle over me.

The great thing about city living is that you could walk anywhere and buy anything. In our rough and tumble old neighborhood, it was not only legal items available for purchase, but a great assortment of other "stuff" too.

We were always fixing something, be it our family car with 300,000 miles on it, or repairing something in our old house at 182 Belmont Avenue in Haledon, New Jersey.

The old house was beloved, but it had some of the worst plumbing on the face of the Earth.

And wires, and roof, and boiler, and foundation, and so on, and so forth. You name it and the house had troubles with it.

His 1964 Putter Classic Model 200 family car was very much beloved, but my goodness, it was a repair a week, or two, or three or more.

In the quest to repair, patch, fix, and maintain, we were constantly walking to fetch supplies for our various repair missions. Our jaunts around the neighborhood remain etched in my mind forever. The old man could walk at such a brisk pace, his long legs carrying him in great strides; almost a slow trot would be an accurate description of his gait. As a little kid, I would struggle to keep up, my little legs scampering along the city sidewalks, often having to break into a run to catch up to the fast pace of my father.

My father would turn and check on me and see that I was lagging behind and he would smile, wave, and yell, "C'mon, shake ya little ass! We gotta get to the hardware store before they close."

I would run and catch up and fall behind once more. Then, run a little more. As I grew taller and stronger, I would walk faster, cover more ground in longer strides, walk more, and run less. Then, as I grew even more, I could easily keep pace, until finally, I had to slow down and hide the fact that the old man was falling behind me.

Natural progression.

Simple, yet such profound memories.

Now, I long for and wish with all my heart to be able to walk up a city street with the old man once more.

I watched the old chap, "Wobble Ass" into the distance and I realized that I had arrived at the front door of our office building. Yes, indeed, what a memorable walk, filled with layers of emotions, and I wondered exactly how many more times that I would make that same jaunt.

"Good morning, Joey," I said with a wave to the lobby security officer as I made my way to the elevators.

"Hey, Pastor Paul! Good weekend? Missed you a few days last week," Joey asked and commented while looking over at me.

"Yes, I took off work for a few days, and yes, I had a great weekend! Thank you. How about you?" I asked, as the elevator doors slowly closed.

Joey nodded, smiled, and just before the doors closed, Joey said, "It was great. Lotsa beer."

Before Joey, there was Hank, Fred, Timmy, and I forget the rest of the names of the other guys. Lobby security officers, the daily walks down the city streets, parking mayhem and the office. All coming to an end after so many years because over the weekend, I wrote a letter to the Governing Board of the Northeast Lutheran District, advising the board of my plan to retire as soon as a replacement bishop was selected, installed, and trained in their duties.

Oh yes, and I also proposed marriage to the lovely Rose Rose Redmond, and she accepted. As I mentioned, life is full of twists and turns.

Last Wednesday, in a heartfelt meeting when Rose stopped by to visit me, we opened our hearts, bared our souls, and finally confessed what we knew was the truth for a very long time and that was that we were hopelessly and madly in love. After both losing our beloved spouses, and our mutual best friends years earlier and being lonely for too long, it was amazing in finally admitting the truth that we knew existed in our hearts for a very long time.

Maybe forever.

After our remarkable meeting, I scribbled a note with some vague and strange details to Martha, who, as I recall, had taken a long lunch in order to leave us in privacy. I left the note on Martha's desk and then, in haste, Rose and I left the office. First, we stopped by a jewelry store and we picked out an incredible engagement ring. Then we had lunch and drinks at an exclusive restaurant here in the downtown area, where I formally proposed and then we took a limousine back to our townhouse. We spent the rest of the day, evening, and weekend making love like wild baboons.

Now, it was Monday; it was late May, and it was a

glorious day. Full of sunshine and gentle breezes. I kept looking out the window and reminding myself of how nice a day it was out there.

I sat at my desk in my office and waited for the arrival of dear Martha, in order for me to explain where this is all going, what it all means, and to face the music. I did not answer her cell phone calls over the last few days because; I was, well, let's just say, very busy. In my feeble defense, I did explain in the note that I was taking a few days off and then left the rest of the details exceedingly vague.

Unless I was away on business or visiting churches and with pastors, I usually beat Martha into the office. Especially so on Monday mornings or as Martha preferred to label Monday, "Cold, Stark, Bleak, Reality Day."

The telltale rattle of the front door told me what the telltale rattle of the front door told me countless times before, and that was to signal the arrival of Ms. Martha Wiggins.

I gripped the arms of "Old Sparky."

I mean my office chair.

The same familiar sounds ran as if they were music in my ears. Footsteps, her desk drawer opening, car keys tossed in the drawer, more footsteps and a loud sigh, followed by a run of the faucet in the sink in the kitchenette, and then the sound of Martha making coffee. I was primarily a tea drinker, but I always made coffee for dear Martha. Now I was going to hear it very loudly because I forgot to make the coffee. I forgot because I was staring out the window too much this morning while still thinking of Rose and our "time" together.

Specifically, the wild baboon analogy time.

The countdown begins . . . five, four, three, two, and one.

"Ya would think that my lover boy of a boss would at least, after not showing up for days and days and ignoring my telephone calls, make the friggin' coffee on Cold, Stark, Bleak, Reality, Day. But, noooooo, not for his faithful and loyal assistant of who knows how many years! You will need to make your own cup of tea! I am making only *my coffee* in an evil, selfish, and wretched display of tilted and warped revenge."

The smell of fresh-brewed coffee filled the office air. I decided to wait this one out and face the music in a few minutes. The new whiz-bang coffee brewer whoosie made a cup of coffee in no time flat.

Within a few minutes, Martha appeared in the doorway to my office, a cup of coffee in her one hand and in the other hand. She held the note that I had scribbled to her last week. She also wore a new dress, a new pair of shoes, and draped over her arm was a designer purse. I must say that Martha looked stunning. Her shoulder-length brown hair was fresh and sparkly, her brown eyes reflected amorously in the light of the office, and while Martha had put on a few pounds over the years, she still had a nice, curvy figure. She looked beautiful. Without saying a single word, Martha walked over to the guest chair in front of my desk; she pulled out the chair, sat in it and then placed the cup of coffee and the designer purse on the edge of the desk.

"Good morning, dear Martha. How was your weekend?"

"Forget that small talk, lover boy. To quote the legend known as your old man, 'What the hell is this bullshit?'"

Martha held up the note, and I went to say something, but Martha held her hand up, interrupted me and said, "Wait. Hold on. Let me read it aloud so we are on the same page."

Martha comically cleared her throat and then proceeded to read my note.

"Hi, Martha. Gone for the rest of the day. If you come back, then I hope you had a nice lunch. I sure as hell did. I will call you tomorrow or whenever, but I will be taking a few days off. Hell, I do not care. Take another long, liquid lunch and hang out with Jennifer. Put it all on my tab. Go and purchase a new dress, new shoes, and a new purse. All on me. I will explain. Thank you for you!"

She then placed the note on my desk; she stood up and waved a hand rather seductively over her new dress to display how awesome the dress was. I did not say a word, but nodded in recognition of the finery of threads on display in front of me. Not to mention how glorious Martha looked in the new dress. Martha then held each foot up to display her new shoes and then grabbed the new purse, opened it, and pulled out a handful of credit card receipts. As she set each one of them on my desk in front of me, Martha explained each one of them.

"First, lunch and hard-core alcohol at The Elusive Lion Public House on Wednesday. Then ditto for Thursday, and then lunch and then dinner, with Jennifer on Friday, as we sucked down the seemingly endless, top-shelf, martinis on your tab and waited with bated breath for an update from, lover boy. An update that never arrived. You must have had poor cell service, or a drained battery. Ha! I bet you drained your battery in more ways than one! We also each took taxi cabs back to our homes because Brad worked late and could not pick us up. Jennifer and I were both three sheets to the wind. You paid for those fares too."

I smiled, but did not say a word. I could tell' that the firing squad still had many more bullets left.

Another receipt came out of the endless cavity of her new purse, followed by more receipts and explanations, "This one is for the dress and shoes, and then, Jennifer and I went up and down every, single, women's fashion store in downtown Newark to find this purse. It cost you a fortune."

I leaned over to try to see the amount on the receipt, but Martha folded it over so I could not see the details.

"Jennifer and I could not decide what color we liked the best, so we bought one of each. Four in total. Two for her and two for me."

Martha smiled, brushed her hair back, and then smoothed her dress out and sat back down in the chair. She crossed her legs, picked up the cup of coffee and took a sip while still coyly smiling at me.

"Oh yes, good morning, Pastor Paul. Welcome to Cold, Stark, Bleak, Reality, Day. By the way, this coffee is marvelous. Soooo, much better when I make it."

"Indubitably," I finally said a word while picking up the receipts and thumbing through them. "Dear Martha, I think that the note specifically states, a lunch, and a purse. As in the singular, form, not plural. Pretty sure, there is no dinner listed here."

"Tough luck, lover boy. You also wrote to hang out with Jennifer. Therefore, I am invoking the hang out clause as allowance to buy dinner and some drinks and gifts for Jennifer too. You left the door, or should I say the line of credit, wide open, and Jennifer and I walked right in. Despite our profound friendship, Jennifer, will not tell me, but she knows some deep, dark secrets about you and can describe in great and in glorious detail, well, let's just say, certain . . . stuff of yours. Apparently, the details of this stuff are quite amazing and rather distinctive. So ya best to go with the flow on this one."

"I guess you are right. Oh well, anyway, nice purse, dress, and the shoes are very nice too. The dress looks beautiful on you. Glorious."

"Bet ya amazing ass it does. I had Joey keeling over in the lobby down there. I thought he would drop dead when I made my breasts bounce a little in front of him. I wore a light-duty bra on purpose today to provoke some extra action from the twins. Anyway, thank you for the line of credit and never, ever, sign your name on your personal credit card that you gave me for emergency use. You will go to jail right away. By the way, once you give me the inside scoop on what is going on and when the wedding date is, then we are going over to The Elusive Lion for lunch and more hammering. Jennifer and I figure if we get you loaded that you will spill the beans on some hot details of the weekend. Years of pent-up lust equals some major bed rattling. So?"

Martha leaned forward, placed both of her elbows on my desk, placed her head in her hands, and playfully and rapidly batted her eyes at me. I sighed deeply. I guess we had worked together forever. Martha knew EVERYTHING. I could not hide ANYTHING. So much for my big plans for an announcement.

I smiled and said, "The wedding is in October. Rose is going to ask you to be a bridesmaid. How did you know?" Martha leaned back in the chair and for the first time this morning, her comical side left her and I saw tears forming in her eyes at the confirmation of the news. She gathered her composure, grabbed the box of tissues on my desk, and pulled one out.

With a dab of her eyes, she answered my question, "Oh, Pastor Paul, it was so easy. The news of Rose and you being in love is such old news. Everyone knew it for a long time. Ever since Mrs. Henson and Mr. Redmond Junior left this world, you could not keep your eyes off each other. In fact, honestly, I think Rose has always loved you. Her love for you is the worst kept secret ever. I knew by the look in Rose's eyes when she came to see you last week. Why do you think I left you two alone? Rose finally came to claim her man. We all knew it. And who could blame her? What woman does not fall in love with you and want to marry you? Count me in that group too. What the hell, I will lay my card's face up."

I smiled and said, "I love you too, Martha."

"Oh yeah, ya do, but not the way that I wanted you to. But anyway, enough of this heart fluttering bullshit. What does this mean for us and for me?"

I knew it was no time to fudge anything or try more comic relief, so I too, set my cards on the table and told

Martha, "I wrote a letter to the board and told them I was going to retire, whenever they could fill my position. I will, of course, recommend that you stay on in your same position and advise them. . . ."

Martha was shaking her head and making a motion for me to stand up and walk over to her. She stood up and opened her arms up to give me a hug. I stood up, walked over to her, and we warmly hugged. I could hear her sobbing and felt her tears dripping on my neck. We did not say a word for a very long time; instead, we just gently rocked together and warmly hugged.

Layers of emotion.

Finally, Martha spoke in a low voice, just above a whisper, "I wish you all the love and luck in the world. You both deserve it. Rose is the luckiest gal in the world and you are a very lucky man, too. After what you both have been through over the years, my goodness, it is no wonder that God brought you together. To find a love like the two of you have is amazing."

We separated, and I took my fingers and wiped her tears off her cheeks.

She forced a smile and said, "Look at me, crying like a boo-boo. I have to tell you that I could never work for any other bishop or pastor after you, Pastor Paul. Never. Ever. There is only one, Pastor Paul. My goodness, all we have been through over these many years. It is like an epic, damn novel that the author cannot figure out how to end the book. However, I guess, the author finally figured it out, and the end is now in sight. Thinking about it, the new guy might make shittier coffee than you do and most likely will be short, bald, fat, and have bad breath, and a flat ass. Who the hell am I gonna lust after now? The new guy would fire me in an hour. One cuss word and out the door, old Martha would go."

I laughed and hugged her again.

"What the hell are you going to do with retirement other

than make Rose the happiest and luckiest woman in the world while you wear out mattresses? Lemme guess, you are going to write your books like a mad demon. I would use a more Martha-like term that you will write like a blankety-blank, but even if we are short-timers and soon to no longer have a boss and worker relationship, nonetheless, the bishop title, I will stick with mad demon."

"Thank you for that choice of words. Yes, I am going to write, love, travel, and do all the things that we should have done so long ago. How about you?"

"Well, Brad's contracting business is booming, so I will work for him doing the office work and that boring filing and paperwork bullshit. I guess we can reignite our love life, too. What the hell, he ain't you, but he ain't all that bad. I do love him dearly with all of my heart and soul, and even though he has a big beer belly, his ass is not too flat. Sometimes, a woman needs a handle to hold on to ya know. Our mattress is a little lumpy, so we will try the floor a few times."

Oh, my dear Martha had no filter.

She motioned for another hug, and we wrapped our arms around each other.

I heard her crying once more, and I asked her while we hugged, "How long have we been working together? Do you know exactly?"

"Hell, if I know, just too damn long. Too gloriously long, and now, I have one last request before we go and meet Jennifer."

I looked at my watch and said, "Okay, but they do not open until eleven."

"Oh, bullshit, Jennifer will sneak us in the back door like she does for all the hard-core alkies. It is time for some major celebrations! You and Rose are finally together! Jennifer and Martha, along with thousands of other women, will cry in disappointment but they will eventually get over it. And retirement, finally. No one has earned it more. Honestly, no one. No more bullshit calls and stupid emails from confused pastors and crazy salespersons trying to sell us plastic crosses that glow in the dark!"

I sure loved Martha Wiggins.

I nodded while saying, "Works for me. Work can wait. We are short timers now. What is the request?"

"For me to call you, Paul, from now on in our lives together. I mean, just because we will not see each other every day and work together does not mean that you are getting rid of me in your life. It ain't that easy to do. I am like a fly in the house. It will be so sexy just to say your name and will seem as if we are intimate in my mind."

I screwed my mouth up like a corkscrew at her comment and Martha quickly stepped in and clarified her comment, "I did say in *my mind.* Not yours. Only a woman who has worked with you, side-by-side and inhaled your amazing man smell for all of these years would understand. So, is it okay for me to drop the pastor title?"

"Of course. Sure, Martha. It is fine. From now on, it is, Paul," I said with a smile.

Martha smiled too. She stepped back, cleared her throat and rolled her eyes. With a deep sigh and breath, she lowered her voice into a faux, sexy growl and said, "Thank you, Paul."

It was hilarious, and I bent over and gently kissed each of Martha's cheeks.

I loved me some Martha Wiggins.

Martha fixed her hair, pushed up at her generous breasts until the twins almost popped out of her neckline, then she released them. She adjusted her brassiere and clapped her hands together while saying, "Okay, I am good now. I can die in glory now. Let's go get hammered. I wonder if The Elusive Lion has a shower in the back that I could use. A very cold, shower."

It was March of the following year after Rose and I married, and it was early on a Saturday evening. I was flipping through the remote control on the television, trying to find the hockey game, when the telephone rang. Rose was in the kitchen whipping up a gourmet delight for dinner, and she picked up the telephone.

It was difficult for me to hear, but after what seemed as if it were a few minutes, I heard Rose say, "Oh no. Oh no. Yes, he is here. I will get him and we will be there as soon as we can."

Now, I was on full alert and I hustled into the kitchen to see Rose's face flush with shock and her slowly hanging up the telephone.

"Rose? Darling? What is going on?"

"It is, dear Martha, Paul. That was, Bradley. Martha has had a massive heart attack. She is in the County General Hospital. They are going to do a quad bypass on her right now. The doctors told Bradley that it is hit or miss if Martha will make it out of the surgery or not."

Oh no, not this time, God. Not again. Not dear Martha. Not now. We are going to have some serious negotiating over this one, Lord.

"I will get dressed," was all that I said.

My black suit and pastor's collar hung in the master closet on a separate hanger. It was as if it was a fireman's turnout gear waiting for an alarm to go off and be ready for action. I dressed and slipped the wooden cross on the cloth lanyard over my head.

Rose and I were there within an hour. We met with Bradley, who told us that Martha was in surgery right now. Their three boys were all there, and they all looked at me with anguish and an intense worry in their eyes.

Bradley added that, "The doctors said it was very serious and that they hoped for the best."

"Bradley, boys, my lovely, Rose, please, I need to excuse myself, find the chapel and pray alone. Then, we will pray together. I will be right back."

Of course, I had been in this particular hospital, as well

as so many others, more times than I could count and even though I was now retired, nurses, doctors, and workers, still waved to me in the hallways and said, "Hello, Pastor Paul."

I waved back to every one of them.

I found the chapel, knelt in a pew on the prayer rail, and prayed, "Lord in Heaven, hear my prayer. Straight talk, now Lord. Forgive me. As the old man would tell me right now, ask humbly, Paul, but tell it as it is. I will and I am. It seems as if Pastor Paul John Henson always arrives here at this same place. To the same struggle where an Earthly loved one is on the edges of entering the Gates of Heaven. While I remain faithful, I remain in your service, and I acknowledge how poor a servant and radical a sinner that I have been, I pray for this one time, for this person to remain here with us. Dear Martha has worked so long and so hard in your service too, a faithful servant who now has a chance to enjoy her life, her husband's love and their family. Together. Please Lord, I humbly pray for Martha to stay here with us . . . with all the people who love her and need her. I need her too, Lord. I need her for her love, her humor, her forthrightness, and for her extraordinary friendship. Her family needs her for the same reasons. This Earthly world needs Martha Wiggins too, because the world is a much better place because of Martha Wiggins. Binky, Harry, Sky Blu, Maria, my brother-in-law, my parents, the Hobnobbers, my other dear friends, and all of our loved ones, with you in your Kingdom, not to mention the twists and turns of my love for Renee. I cannot lose, dear Martha. Not yet. I humbly beseech you, Lord, for the plan to be different. Very different. I am not sure that I can dig far enough into my soul right now to lose Martha and watch her family lose her extraordinary love, too. Thank you. Lord, hear my prayer."

I breathed deeply and then continued with the Lord's Prayer, "Our Father, who art in Heaven. . .."

I walked out of the chapel, back through the familiar hallways, and returned to meet Rose, Bradley, and the boys. They all studied my eyes, and I felt very confident. My soul was calm, and I was quite sure that The Lord had heard my prayer.

"Please, let us make a circle here in this waiting room and hold hands, and we will all pray. I smiled and extended my hand. Rose immediately took my hand in hers, and Bradley took my other hand while signaling the boys. There was a middle-aged couple sitting in the waiting room, holding hands and watching us very carefully. To say they had a look of concern on their faces was a terrible understatement.

I looked over at them, smiled, and asked, "Are you waiting for news on a loved one in surgery, too?"

They looked at each other, and the man nodded first, followed by his female companion.

The woman spoke, "Yes, my mother is having surgery. It is very serious."

I asked, "Would you like to join us in prayer?"

The woman spoke once again, "Yes, but we are Catholic and we are not sure of your denomination."

I smiled and asked, "Does it really matter? We are all under God. Please, let us pray."

They nodded fervently and jumped up, held their hands out, and joined the group.

"What is your mother's name?" I asked.

"Maria," the woman said, with tears welling in her eyes. When I heard the name Maria, I felt a chill running up and down my spine and while quickly recovering, I said, "Shall we pray for, Maria and for Martha? Father in Heaven. . .."

After prayer, the agonizingly long wait settled in. A few hours later, a surgeon in scrubs appeared and looked around the room and asked, "Maria's family?"

They slowly rose to their feet, and I held my breath and felt Rose's grip on my hand tighten.

The conversation was low, but it was loud enough for me to hear, "She is going to be fine."

Then the tears of joy followed. Before they went to see their loved one, they hustled over to me. I stood up. The man extended his hand and graciously thanked me, and the woman gave me a hug and thanked me too.

I smiled, blessed them, made the sign of the cross over them both and said, "Go in peace and in thanks, to, The Lord."

While watching them walk away with their arms wrapped around each other in comfort and in love, I knew that everything would work out wonderfully for them and for Maria. The peace in my heart told me so.

We sat in silence for another hour or so. I prayed silently. Rose held my hand tightly and with my other hand, I held Bradley's hand. The boys . . . they were all grown now, young, strong, handsome men, and to think that I baptized all of them and I knew them all when they were in diapers.

They all had tears in their eyes.

It was taking so long.

Why was it taking so long?

Events, words, moments that Martha and I shared over all of our many years together ran endlessly within my mind.

Finally, a surgeon in blue scrubs appeared, followed by an operating room nurse and then another doctor. I studied their eyes for any clues, but there were none. Rose's grip tightened, and she began to sob. I wrapped my arms around her as Bradley and the boys stood up.

"Martha Wiggin's family and friends . . . I assume," the first surgeon said.

Now, we all stood up and rushed over as Bradley almost shouted, "We are here. I am her husband and these are our boys, our pastor, and his wife. They are actually our friends too!"

The doctor smiled, placed his hand on Bradley's shoulder, and I felt the glory and compassion of God.

The Grace.

The power of Heaven.

The glory of it all.

"Martha is going to be fine. She is going to be fine. Martha has a long road ahead of her with some rehab and from now on, eating a proper diet and performing various exercises, but she is going to be fine." Tears of joy streamed down all of our faces, and I gently kissed the lovely Rose's cheek.

"That is one tough woman. We almost lost her twice, but she fought back. I guess," the doctor stalled and then looked at me, my collar, and then at each of us, and he smiled, as did the nurse and the other surgeon, "I guess, there was some heavy-duty prayer going on out here and God heard your prayers."

"There sure was, doc," Bradley said as he held his arms out for all of us to gather in while adding, "lots of prayer and love too."

We slipped into the room to see Martha, but of course, she was out of it and never knew we were there. I prayed over her for thankfulness and praise to The Lord.

Rose and I returned a few days later, when Bradley told us that Martha was up, while she was slowly moving around, eating a little and asking for Rose and me to come and see her. We walked in the room, holding a dozen roses as a gift. Martha looked up, and she smiled widely. She looked weak and a little frail, but her color was returning to her face and I saw that familiar, devious lick in her eyes.

"Get your handsome face and glorious ass over here and give me a kiss, Paul. The roses are all fancy and pretty and stuff, but I want a big, old smooch right on the kisser too. No little bullshit pecks on the cheeks. I want a wet one! After this hospital bullshit, I earned it. I hope it does not make my heart conk out, but if it does, then it will be worth it!"

Rose laughed and Bradley said with exuberance, "I want to kiss him too for putting up with you for all of these years."

I leaned in and gave Martha a gentle kiss on her lips, and then I gently hugged her as she playfully fanned her face. Martha then happily waved for Rose, the boys, and for her husband to join us in kisses and a group hug.

"I love you, dear Martha," I said to her.

Tears ran down her cheeks as she answered, "I love you too, dear Paul. I could never leave you first. Think about it. I would haunt your handsome ass every, single, day. Float around the room, yell at you and tell you all the things that you are doing wrong and how terrible that your coffee is. I would be the worst ghost ever!"

"You would. No doubt.

Martha leaned back against her pillow, and her eyes widened while she waved her hands in the air. It seemed as if Martha was excited about something.

Her voice rose in volume and increased in excitement as Martha spoke, "I have waited impatiently for you to visit. It has been so glorious sitting here thinking about something that happened to me. An experience of such glory. I have been so anxious to tell you, Paul. I saw the glory of Heaven. I swear that I did. Not like the time we got loaded at The Elusive Lion and I told you that I saw Saint Michael in your beer mug. This was real! I swear it was! It was like one of those crazy, whacked out books ya see in the bookstores. You know, somebody claims to see angels and glowing prophets with fire in their eyeballs and other stuff while on their deathbed. The Path to Heaven or some other bullshit is usually the title of the book. I had this glorious dream, honest. I saw everyone . . . my parents, my grandparents, my family members, all standing and smiling at me."

I looked over to Rose, Bradley, and the boys, and they all were listening intently. It seems as if no one had heard this testimony before now.

Martha continued, "Then, I saw Dave Sharp and Bishop Von Houten, and Rabbi Goldberg and Mrs. Henson and Mr. Redmond Junior, too! Then, Ronzo and all the gang. They all stood smiling and waving at me! It was grand and indescribably gorgeous. Then, out of the angelic haze, your father and mother appeared. Dear Mum was holding the old man's hand and your father smiled and spoke, 'Martha, cuz, I am, the old man, I can say this here and get away with it.' He put his hands on his hips and screwed his mouth up, and with that classic stance and pose, the old man said, 'What the hell is this bullshit? Ya ain't supposed to be here yet. Get ya ass on back there and take care of things. Our son, Rose, and your husband, your boys, and family all need you. The world needs you, Martha Wiggins. We will see you someday, but today ain't the day!' I woke up, saw the bright lights of a room, and realized that I was still alive. Then, I swear, I heard your voice, Paul, loud and clear in my ear, I swear that I could hear you say, this Earthly world needs Martha Wiggins too, because the world is a much better place because of Martha Wiggins. I swear that it was your voice."

Now, I really knew the power and the glory of God.

The timing of all of this was remarkable. A few days earlier, I confessed to Rose that I thought that after all of these years that I was incorrect. The ghosts that I swore that haunted me since I was a little boy were not actually ghosts after all. I came to realize that they were actually angels and not ghosts that surrounded me in my life. Rose agreed and now I knew that we were correct.

In gratitude, I warmly embraced Martha as we all sobbed tears of joy.

Layers of emotions captured us.

"I am glad you knew better than to argue with the old man, because you needed to get back here soon. The world really is a better place because of Martha Wiggins. No way were we going to lose you. No way. Love is God's greatest gift to us and you, dear Martha, are pure love."

"Does that mean that I can have another kiss, Paul? Can Rose, Brad, and the boys look the other way so I can grab your glorious backside when we kiss? I mean, c'mon now, it is just'a little, harmless, squeeze."

I sure loved Martha Wiggins.

Glancing over at the clock in my office told me the horrible news. It was four in the morning. Time escaped me once more. I saved the file and backed it up onto two backup drives. I cannot risk losing work to electronic whoosie malfunctions.

A very long time ago, Rose had stuck her head in the door after her shower and my wife graciously blew me a kiss goodnight.

Hours and hours ago.

I had to keep typing.

This memory had to come out and jump into the pages of this book.

It just had too.

I stood up, stretched, picked up my empty Scotch glass, walked over to the wet-bar and placed the glass on the counter of the bar. I left the cool, blue, L.E.D. lights of the bar on, but shut off my office lights and made my way to the master bedroom.

Rose was sound asleep, so I crept quietly by her without turning a light on and made my way into the master bathroom. I stripped down and climbed into the shower. Wow, the warm water felt so good. What a long day of writing that was.

A few seconds later, the door to the shower flew open, and I almost jumped out of my skin!

Rose stood there in all her glorious, naked wonder,

smiling at me as she climbed into the shower and she said, "So, big guy, you wanna swap some spits and make some wild whoopee in the shower?"

The lovely Rose was amazing in every way and I do mean in every way!

"Hell yeah, I do!"

I opened my arms and as the water hit us both, Rose laughed and said, "Warning, we are gonna need more boxes of tissues and jars of menthol rub."

Yes, indeed, love is God's greatest gift to us.

Along with tissues and menthol rub.

THE END

The Last Letter

Beloved Wife,

While I enjoyed a rather intense education in writing and composition while in seminary and in my university studies, I never really took any creative writing courses. Seminary was so different as far as writing instruction is concerned. It is, of course, all about sermons and religious dissertations. Certainly, a far cry from the *Adventures of Harry and Paul*. My goodness, so far away, yet when I first typed out those, now classic, opening words to *The Time Bomb in The Cupboard* and it sent a shiver down my spine to do so, I knew that I had to continue to write on.

'My best buddy growing up was Harry M. Redmond Junior. Even as a little kid and as a teenager, he was loud, bombastic, friendly, and outgoing. He had a mischievous side, but for the most part, he stayed out of trouble. He was a great friend to hang with; no one was more fun.'

Now, my heart flutters and tears fall from my eyes when I recall your words, when you leaned in and read what I typed.

Your words still resound within my mind, bouncing back and forth off the sidewalls of my brain.

"Oh my, twenty-seven, that is quite a way to start. I think you have summed it all up already."

That might have been the most accurate observation that you ever conveyed to me, dear Binky.

A few weeks ago, on a wild and strange whim, I did enroll in some creative writing course at an adult education night school, conducted at a local university in Wayne, New Jersey. The tag line for the course was, "A perfect writing course for experienced writers as well as those writers that are first beginning their writing ventures."

The instructor was some stuffy gal, with horrible perfume that smelled similar to turpentine mixed with stale beer, bright red lipstick, and one of the worst hairstyles that I have ever seen. Her flaming red hair looked like an upside-down ice cream cone on her head. A red ice cream cone. She wore a bright red dress and white sneakers with nude stockings. My goodness, she looked as if she was a pinup gal for some flash fiction periodical from the 1950s.

Her credentials were impressive enough, even a best seller or two under her belt. It seems as if nowadays all these authors have best sellers.

Except for me.

Anyway, I know in my heart, your research would have told me to avoid it, and uncovered beforehand that it was a waste of my time and money, but I thought that I might learn something. You know, steer me in a different direction from my current writing and perhaps open new horizons of my writing. I remained incognito in the class, never told anyone what my many professions are or were, or the fact that I now had twenty or so books under my belt. The class was a mixture of young persons and housewives wanting to write their dream book, along with a few older men who looked as they recently retired and wanted to do something to get away from their wives. On the other hand, perhaps, their wives had signed them up to get rid of them. Or a combination thereof.

Well, the instructor's opening statement was, "Whether it is nonfiction or fiction that we want to write, we as writers, tend to write about our own experiences, people that you met, or know, and of what happened to come true in your life. In fictional work, even if we twist the facts around, we tend to lean on our own lives for inspiration."

I thought to myself, "Really? Bloody well! No kidding. A friggin' well-worn adage is the opening statement by the instructor to her class. Really?"

To quote the old man, "What the hell is this bullshit?"

I pretended that I had to go to the restroom, left, and never went back.

They probably never even missed me.

Forget any new horizons because I am perfectly happy to hang out on the old horizons.

I returned to my office, typed like a mad demon, and finished these chronicles in a week or two. It was a glorious time for me to write these and expel it out of my soul.

Now, I am not too sure what is next for me to write. Maybe I will write Chronicles Part Two?

Maybe.

In fact, I have shared so much profoundly personal information here within these pages and stories that I am not sure that I will even publish this manuscript.

I do not know, and honestly, I am not even concerned with the ultimate fate of this work.

In retrospect, I guess time will eventually tell, and even if I do not publish this manuscript or carry on with my writings, maybe someone else in our family will discover these writings and publish them in the future.

Right for now, I keep writing.

It is so mysterious, a song on the radio, a spoken word, the wind blowing in the trees, our grandchildren's laughter, or Rose's smile, and off I go again on some wild idea. The fingers fly on the keyboard and my mind whirls. Yet, someday, it will all stop. I know it will.

Until then, I will write on, dear Binky. I will write on. I will know when to stop because it will be where I began.

Where we begin is often not far from where we end.

Where we rest our heart and our love is to where we will always return.

Please, let me try to type it correctly from memory.

"The sunrays left and the breeze of the early evening carried the whispers away. There is always a special wind right before and right after the sunset. It is very, very special.

The whispers gradually faded, and they disappeared into a gentle evening breeze, but tomorrow night on the sunset breeze, they will return once again, because the night always comes.

Yes, indeed, in this glorious life and world, the night always comes."

And that, my beloved wife, is where we all began.

Love Always,

#27

Epilogue

I opened the door to the safe and carefully peered inside at the contents. It took me a few moments of sifting through the contents, but in a short amount of time, I found the little box that I wanted. With a smile, I reached for it, and then I sat on my backside on the floor in front of the safe.

The little box seemed to glow in my hands. I carefully opened the cover and there it was. The silver locket. It glowed and glistened, and the power and the glory of it seemed to make my soul ache. On the other hand, was it my heart that ached, or was it both? I felt some tears welling up in my eyes as I absorbed the love contained within the silver locket. I closed the cover, stood up, and while carrying the little box in my hands, I made my way over to my writing desk. I set the jewelry box next to my laptop and with an eye on it; I took a deep breath and began to type:

My Dearest Sarah,

If you are reading this and holding a small jewelry box in your hands that contains a fantastic silver locket, then Grandpa is off in Heaven having a grand old time. Never forget that I am always with you. Until the end of all time.

The silver locket has all the power and glory contained within it that you will ever need. A very special woman who your grandpa loved very much gave it to me. After your grandmother left us, your grandfather had a very difficult time of it while trying hard to recover. Loneliness was not the only painful emotion that caused me suffering, but it might have been one of the strongest. This special woman arrived at a time in both of our lives where we needed to share each other's life and love. No doubt, our reunion and love were part of God's plan. I am not the least bit ashamed in admitting that I loved her too, with all my body, heart, and soul. Her name was Maria Grace Ellsworth, and she was very much as you are.

Gorgeous inside and outside.

Maria had a very difficult time of it in life, and she left me, and this world, all too soon to become a saint in Heaven, but she never forgot that her mother gave her the silver locket in the spirit of love. Just before Maria died, she gave it to me and now; I give it to you. In the spirit of love. Hold it near and dear to your heart, feel the love and power and when the time finally comes in some far-off distant time and place, then you will pass it off to someone you love and the power and the glory will perpetuate. Just as the love of God continues now and always.

Until the end of all time.

Love is God's greatest gift to us and who or what we cherish the most in our lives is where we always hide our hearts, dear Sarah. Hide your heart within the silver locket, and your love will fill the entire world. Now, and until the end of all time.

Love Always,

Grandpa

I saved the file and labeled it, then hit the "PRINT" button. The telltale sound of the printer printing out the words on a piece of paper rattled along next to me. I reached over, pulled the letter out of the printer, and checked it over. It looked good, so I took my best pen, a pen that writes smooth and glides across the paper like my ice skates on the ice. I signed the letter, then opened a desk drawer and pulled out an envelope. With a few quick folds of the letter, I slipped the letter inside and I sealed the envelope. With a stroke of the same pen, I wrote, "To, Sarah Howard. This letter goes along with the small black, jewelry box," on the front of the envelope.

I had to write this letter, just in case. I picked up the box, walked across the room and carefully replaced it in the safe and placed the letter with the box. With a loud thud, I closed the door. Now, the emotions and the memories caught up with me.

These chronicles seemed so endless.

They chased me through time.

I placed my hand on the door of the safe, wiped away a tear, and mumbled, "I will always be here. In the dark and in the light. The happy times and the sad times, the desperate times, always and forever, I am always here. God will not allow me to be anywhere else."

"For where your treasure is, there will your heart be as well."

The Bible

(The Gospel of Saint Matthew, 6:21 King James Version.)

ABOUT THE AUTHOR

If you ask Paul John Hausleben, he will tell you that he is not an author, he is just a storyteller. His mission is to continue to write and tell stories to warm your heart, make you laugh, and sometimes make you cry, just a little. Most of all, he deals in memories, and helps you to remember the good times of your own life, and the special people who touched you along the way. Paul was born and raised in Paterson, and then nearby Haledon, New Jersey, and began writing at an early age. He revisited a writing career later in his life, and he now is the author of a number of novels, compilations, short stories and audio and video works. Most of his work touches upon nostalgic remembrances of simpler times, and tells the stories of heartfelt, humorous, and special human relationships. Other than writing, among many careers both paid and unpaid, he is a former semi-professional hockey goaltender, a music fan and music reviewer, an avid sports fan, photographer and amateur radio operator. He now resides in Somewhere, U.S.A., but his heart always remains along Belmont Avenue in good old Paterson, and Haledon, New Jersey.

Other Work by Mr. Paul John Hausleben

The Time Bomb in The Cupboard and Other Adventures of Harry and Paul

The Night Always Comes, Another story from the Adventures of Harry and Paul

Reunion, A sequel to the Night Always Comes and Another story from the Adventures of Harry and Paul

The Autumn Collection

The Christmas Tree and Other Christmas Stories. Tales for a Christmas Evening

Crows on a High Wire

The Miracle Tree, Another story from the Adventures of Harry and Paul

The Summer Collection

Special Edition: The Time Bomb in The Cupboard and Other Adventures of Harry and Paul

Tales of the Quiet Stranger in the Black Hat

Geyer Street Gardens
Beneath the Mask of a Hockey Goaltender
Another story from the Adventures of Harry and Paul

And a few others too!

You may write to the author at ctte27@gmail.com

Published by God Bless the Keg Publishing
Somewhere, U.S.A.

You may write to the publisher at
Godblessthekegpublishing@gmail.com

"Life's simple pleasures are so often the best ones!"

Paul John Hausleben

www.ingramcontent.com/pod-product-compliance
Lightning Source LLC
LaVergne TN
LVHW030911080826
845145LV00010B/2852

9780998630045